D1229103

The Summer Between Us

Andre Fenton

Formac Publishing Company Limited
Halifax

Formac Publishing Company Limited recognizes the support of the Province of Nova Scotia through the Department of Communities, Culture and Heritage. We are pleased to work in partnership with the Province of Nova Scotia to develop and promote our cultural resources for all Nova Scotians. We acknowledge the support of the Canada Council for the Arts, which last year invested $153 million to bring the arts to Canadians throughout the country. This project has been made possible in part by the Government of Canada.

Cover design: Tyler Cleroux
Cover image: Shutterstock

Library and Archives Canada Cataloguing in Publication

Title: The summer between us / Andre Fenton.
Names: Fenton, Andre, 1995- author.
Identifiers: Canadiana (print) 20210390026 | Canadiana (ebook) 20210390034 | ISBN 9781459506817
(softcover) | ISBN 9781459506947 (hardcover) | ISBN 9781459506824 (EPUB)
Subjects: LCGFT: Novels.
Classification: LCC PS8611.E57 S86 2022 | DDC jC813/.6,Äîdc23

Published by:
Formac Publishing
Company Limited
5502 Atlantic Street
Halifax, NS, Canada
B3H 1G4
www.formac.ca

Distributed in Canada by:
Formac Lorimer Books
5502 Atlantic Street
Halifax, NS, Canada
B3H 1G4

Distributed in the US by:
Lerner Publisher Services
241 1st Ave. N.
Minneapolis, MN, USA
55401
www.lernerbooks.com

Printed and bound in Canada.
Manufactured by Friesens Corporation in Altona, Manitoba, Canada in March 2022.
Job #288004

Contents

For the Black and Brown kids trying to find a place in a world that doesn't always feel like it was made for them. This place is so much more illuminating with you in it. This is for you.

CHAPTER 1

Prom Night

Everyone thinks prom night is like the movies. It's less dramatic, trust me. Once you get to the end of high school, you begin to realize there is no secret ending, or a definitive experience. It's multiple choice at best. I can say more often than not, it's a whirlpool that makes you hold your breath. For the past three years, I've been stuck with the feeling of holding in a breath that I wanted anywhere but inside of my chest.

If you're new to this group, let me introduce myself. My name is Adrian Carter. I'm eighteen years old, and I'm graduating high school with honours. I have great friends, and an experience that's similar to yours.

When I was in grade ten, I developed an eating disorder. Guys with eating disorders!? Weird, right? Not really. It's more common than you think. One thing I learned is just because I lost weight, it didn't mean my problems were solved. I was yet to grow into the best parts of myself. I'd like to think that I'm closer than I was before, but the future is still to be determined.

I'm lucky enough to be surrounded by supportive friends, to have had wonderful mentors and to be part of groups like this.

So as my first post as a "mentor" (I'm sorry. That still sounds weird to say), I want to leave you all with this:

You are worthy of the love, healing and support you seek. You always have been and always will be.

Yours truly,

Adrian

I hit enter and finally exhaled. "Not a bad start." My moment of bliss was interrupted by a knock on my door.

"Adrian. Your mother wants photos of you in your suit five minutes ago," Dad called into my room.

"Yeah, one minute." I put on the blazer and took a quick look in the mirror. I had to stop and take a second look. It felt weird. I never really had a suit before. Most of the time, clothes either felt too big or too small. I think what freaked me out the most was knowing that this was a . . .

"Perfect fit," I said out loud. I looked back toward my laptop to see the post already getting some love. When I tried to peek at some replies, I heard a car horn outside.

"Damn, Donny's here early." I shut the laptop. "Don't worry about the pictures, I'll get tons tonight." I opened my door and saw Dad.

"Whoa, whoa, not so fast." Dad blocked the way. It wasn't that I was short, it was just that Dad towered over me. "Look at you. I bet you must be surprised you can fit into one of these, huh?"

I sighed. I really wish he hadn't said that.

"Besides the tie." He pointed. I could tell he was judging me because it was purple, even if he didn't say it.

"Dad, you don't have to —"

"So . . . you hear anything back from Cape Breton University?" He started fixing my tie and making it look worse than before.

"No." I sighed again. "I was wait-listed, remember?"

"I remember." Dad sounded a little disappointed at the news. "Hey, you never know. You could be next on the list if someone drops out. You gotta use that scholarship for something."

My least favourite thing about grade twelve was the idea that we were suddenly supposed to know what we wanted to do with the rest of our lives. Spoiler alert: I didn't. That didn't stop Dad from pressuring me into applying for a business administration program way back in November, and of course, programs like those fill up fast. I applied knowing full well I'd hit the waitlist. What I hadn't expected was that somewhere along the way, I'd find something I was passionate about: working with youth. Last year, Mom had wanted me to help with a group for young men at the library where she works. I was hesitant at first, but next thing I knew, I started to enjoy it. Eventually, I built up the courage to apply for another program at Cape Breton University: community studies. Nothing really says maturity like becoming the person you needed when you were younger.

I never told my parents about it. Just like I hadn't told them I was in an online eating disorder recovery group, or that I even had one. As much as I advocated online, I wasn't ready to speak to my parents about it.

The big reason they were on my back was because I received a scholarship from my high school based on academic achievement and transformation. It's hard to believe I'm the same person who started high school three years ago. That didn't automatically translate into confidence though.

"Yeah, maybe. I mean, who knows? I might not even hear back until next year." I shrugged while walking downstairs. Before I even got to the bottom, I was met face first with a flash.

"Mom?" I rubbed my eyes. "You don't need to use flash indoors."

"Oh, hush," she said, taking another. "I gotta get them while I can. Where's Mel? I want to get her too."

"Trust me, Mom. You'll get enough pictures of me and Mel," I told her.

"Yeah, but she takes poto-roids. It isn't the 1980s. Why doesn't she get a digital camera?"

"Polaroids, Mom. And most people just use their phones these days," I said under my breath.

"I have an answer for that, Ms. Carter." I looked up and saw Donny already making himself comfortable at the kitchen counter. "She's a hipster."

"She isn't a hipster." I shook my head.

"Sure. She just has a hipster name, listens to hipster music and is in a hipster band."

I rolled my eyes almost immediately. It was true — not

the hipster part. Mel was part of a punk band called Brown, Black & Infamous with her friends, Kara, Azra and Jade. They were getting their name out there around Halifax, and Mel was hoping to leave for a tour at the end of the summer, meaning we had a lot to talk about.

"C'mon, Donny. We have work to do." I dragged him outside while he grabbed a cookie from the jar on the kitchen counter.

"You have everything?" I asked as he scoffed it down.

"Yep. Been sitting there since Monday." He opened the trunk. Inside were balloons, a stepladder, tape and a banner which read: *Happy Birthday Mel!*

"You know you're the corniest dude I've ever met, right?" Donny grinned.

"Just shut up. Let's go."

The plan was simple. We were throwing a surprise birthday party for Mel. It seemed easy enough: get the house keys from her dad, grab the supplies and keep her away.

The last part was easy. Azra and Jade took Mel out for dinner while Donny and I planned to meet Kara at her place and set up a surprise before we headed to prom.

When we got to Mel's, there was no sign of Kara, so I sent along a text.

Me: Hey you coming?

There was no reply. I searched for the keys while holding most of the supplies, as Donny had the banner.

"Hurry up," Donny sighed, looking annoyed at me.

"Dude, if I wasn't carrying everything, I'd have it open."

"Yeah, yeah, yeah. Where's Kara?"

"Don't know. She didn't text back." I stuck the key in the lock. Eventually I felt the door unlock and entered the house. It was complete darkness, and I searched aimlessly for the light switch. I found it and turned on the light to see Mel sitting with her feet up on the table, blowing into a birthday kazoo and wearing a cone hat that read: *Birthday Girl*.

I looked over at Donny and mouthed, "Why is she here?" Donny shrugged as Azra walked into the room. "Sorry guys. You know how easily a Gemini can change plans." She shrugged.

"Sounds about right." Mel smiled as she stood up, walking toward me.

"Sorry your plan didn't work out, babe." She kissed my cheek. "I appreciate this so much." She wrapped her arms around me. I smiled and held on. She was in a purple prom dress and had her hair all done up.

"You look really beautiful, Mel," I said in a shy voice.

"You're not so bad either," she observed. "Besides the tie."

"Yeah . . ." I began fidgeting with it again.

"I can help." She took it from my hands and got it done up properly. "You just gotta be a little patient is all."

Jade left the room, and I watched Azra snatch Donny in the background, dragging him upstairs, giving us some alone time before the actual party started.

Mel smiled when she heard the door shut. "I can't believe you put all this together."

"I tried. I mean, you're not exactly easy to surprise." I grinned.

"Don't worry, you're doing great." She pulled me in for a kiss.

"Oh!" I stepped back, thinking out loud. "I have your flower thing."

I reached into my blazer's pocket.

Mel laughed. "My flower thing?"

"Yeah, you know the thing the guy usually puts on their prom date's dress?" I pulled out a plastic case with a purple flower inside.

"Yes. That's called a corsage, Adrian," she laughed.

"Can I?"

"Get over here." She pulled me toward her.

I put the corsage on Mel's dress, and she giggled at my goofy face. Even after three years of being in a relationship, it was only getting better.

"Dammit. Is she already there?" I heard Kara's voice.

Mel snorted. "Yes, Kara, get in here!"

We all sat around in Mel's kitchen eating the cake Kara had brought, that she didn't trust Donny and me to handle. Mel and Kara met at a punk show a couple years back and connected easily.

"How ya feel, Mel?" Jade asked. "Ready to head out?"

"I feel like I just ate an entire cake, and now I have to dance. What is this?" Mel groaned but smiled.

"Girl, you know tonight is gonna be fire. C'mon, we can't be late." Kara got up.

"Ha, we're already an hour and a half late," Mel replied.

"Yeah, and do you really think we wanna miss Donny try his spit game on girls?" Azra said.

Donny shook his head. "Don't roast the man who's driving y'all there."

"That's exactly what we're going to do." Kara laughed.

"I'll ride with Adrian. We'll be right behind you," Mel said.

The band, along with Donny, drove off shortly after. Mel and I sat in her car about to back out until another car came up the driveway.

"Ugh, that's my dad," Mel cut into my thoughts. "Hold on." She took the keys out of the ignition.

I got out of the car with Mel. She drove a purple old school classic Camaro that her dad bought her for Christmas years ago. He always held very high expectations, but Mel wanted to be free and do her own thing. Mel never wanted to be in the elite level class at school. She joined because her dad pressured her to. I knew she resented him because of it.

"Melody!" Mel's father greeted her with an enthusiastic grin. "My girl is all grown up." He pulled her into a hug. Mel sighed and hugged him back.

"What's up, Dad?"

"What's up? It's my girl's birthday, and she's going to prom on the same night." He smiled, then looked over at me. "With Adrian," he added not too enthusiastically.

"Hey, Mr. Woods." I nodded.

"Please, son. You can call me Martin by this point."

"Hey, Martin." I tossed his keys over to him and he caught them.

Mel giggled while I tried to hide my smirk.

"Yes. Hello, Adrian. Give us a minute." He frowned then turned and walked off with Mel.

I wasn't sure what they were talking about, but I watched Mel's shoulders tense up in the distance. As she walked back, I heard her say, "Listen, I just want to enjoy tonight. I'll focus on the rest of my life, starting tomorrow." She grabbed my hand and pulled me along with her.

"Sorry he's such a pain," she said as she got in the driver's seat.

"I don't think he likes me," I replied, shutting the passenger door.

"I don't think he does either. That's just more of a reason to love ya." She hit the gas.

"So . . ." Mel said, eyes still on the road. "Did you think about it?"

Then there's that. Yes, I thought about it. It was honestly a question I wanted to avoid, and we were inching closer and closer to the moment where I'd finally have to confront that elephant in the room.

"Silence? C'mon, scholarship boy."

As happy as Mel was for me, she sort of knew it wasn't where my heart was. Being stuck between a scholarship and a waitlist, the idea of the future was difficult to navigate.

"I'm still thinking on it." I swallowed.

Mel looked disappointed by my response, but she didn't push. She just kept her eyes on the road, focusing on the ride ahead of us.

I tried staying quiet for the rest of the ride, until I saw an envelope on her dashboard. There was a stamp on it and the return address said it was from Toronto.

"Who sent mail?" I asked.

"That was a great post you wrote, by the way," Mel said, changing subjects.

"Wait, you read that too?"

Mel, like me, struggled with an eating disorder in the past. Her mom left after a bad divorce with Martin, and I guess, also like me, she turned to food for a lot of reasons. She was the one who told me about the youth eating disorder group. I'd been part of it for the past two years, but was about to age out of it.

"Of course I did." She grinned. "I might not be active in the group but I still check in. They're lucky you're welcoming the new teenagers."

I smiled after she said that.

When we pulled up to the school parking lot, it was full of students getting photos taken and making their way toward the entrance. Usually the school had prom at a hotel nearby, however this year it happened to be double-booked, meaning the school had to compromise by having our prom in the school's cafeteria. It was supposed to be a fun time, until we saw Donny's car getting towed.

"Where are you going with my car? We were gone for five seconds!" Donny was pulling his hair.

"Sorry, kid. It just got called in while I was nearby. You're not supposed to park here," an older man in overalls said while hopping in the front seat of the tow truck.

"What happened?" I walked up to Donny.

"Me and the girls went up to the entrance with our prom tickets, and next thing I knew Tyler comes up and tells me he seen some guy towing my car." Donny kicked a rock across the parking lot.

"Why? Everyone is parked here." I looked around.

"I have an idea." Jade pointed.

We all looked over to see a black SUV park in the spot where Donny's car had been.

"For future reference, Donny. Don't park in the reserved student union section." Out came the student vice president, Shay, with a smug grin as he strutted toward the entrance.

Donny's jaw dropped. "That piece of sh —"

"Mel, do you still have the keys to the greenhouse?" Kara asked.

"Yeah, in my bag." Mel reached into her purse and fished them out. "Gotta give them back tomorrow."

"Well, I've got a plan," Kara said, as Shay disappeared into the school.

While Donny had a complete meltdown, Kara and Mel returned, dragging a hose toward Shay's SUV.

"Wait, what are you doing?" I asked.

"Letting Shay know that nobody messes with us," Kara told me as she put the hose through a crack in the SUV's window. Of course, Shay was the only eighteen-year-old who had an SUV that I knew of.

"You wanna do the honours, Azra?" Kara asked while Jade shook her head.

"Already ahead of you," Azra said, turning the tap on to let Shay know payback doesn't take long to manifest.

Inside, the DJ played classic tunes and the blue lights made everything feel old-school.

I was drinking fruit punch, standing against the wall, watching Mel laughing and having fun with her pals. Donny stood beside me. He'd finally calmed down after Kara offered him a ride to Bayers Lake the next day to get his car.

"Aren't you gonna dance with Mel?" he asked.

"Probably."

"What are you waiting for?"

"The right moment." I was hiding my face with my cup. Mel was on the other side of the cafeteria, looking at me and making funny faces.

"All right, stand against the wall all night." Donny walked away.

Nobody wanted to be the first to slow dance at prom. It was awkward, and I didn't want to bring any more attention to us than we already had . . . Then I heard, "Adrian Carter would like to dedicate this song to his hipster girlfriend, Melody Woods." I looked up and saw the DJ reading a cue card with Donny laughing in the background.

"Oh no," I gasped as a slow song began to play. Mel laughed like thunder on the other side of the cafeteria.

She walked over to me, grabbed my hands and placed them around her waist.

"What were you waiting for?" she asked.

"Clearly not that." I moved with her toward the centre of the room.

"Well, I think that's the best we're gonna get." She swayed slowly back and forth. The lights went low. I felt so lucky being with Mel, and sharing that moment at prom was going to be something worth remembering.

"You still give me butterflies every now and then," I whispered.

"I can tell." She leaned her head on my chest. "I think it's cute. You're cute."

I rested my chin on her head, and I looked across the room at Kara, Azra and Jade, who were smiling at us. We moved back and forth for a while, and soon other couples did too. Everyone kinda faded together slowly.

"I love you," Mel whispered.

"I love you too," I whispered back.

"Keep saying sweet things," she said.

"Okay," I replied. "Can I ask you something?"

"Sure." Mel buried her face in my chest. I knew she was going to hate me for saying it. She always hated me when I said it, but it was just too funny not to.

"Are you the circular land formation around one end of the ocean?"

Mel sighed, and I knew she rolled her eyes.

"Because I wanna call you bae."

"Ugh. That's the worst!" I heard Azra say to me from nearby.

"She's right. You're the worst." Mel adjusted herself and moved her hands to my shoulders while looking into my eyes.

"I'm vaguely okay."

"Worse than that." She grinned.

"Oh, that's hurtful."

"I know." She giggled.

Moments later, the music stopped, followed by a public service announcement by the DJ.

"To whoever drives a black SUV, it is currently over-flowing with water."

"Time to go." Mel pulled my arm as we all ran outside.

Outside of the school, Shay flipped out as he opened the passenger side door and water poured everywhere.

"Are you kidding me!" He looked over at us and pointed straight at Mel. "You're in charge of the gardens here. This hose is from the greenhouse. Why'd you do this!"

"Eh, don't be a cop next time!" Kara laughed.

Shay wasn't impressed. He stormed right toward us with his finger still pointed at Mel.

"How are you paying for this? With your dad's shitty music shop?" Shay yelled.

Mel took one look at that finger and counted.

"Three . . . two . . . one."

She grabbed it and twisted it backward, causing Shay to screech, then kneed him in the stomach, bringing him to his knees.

"You put that finger in my face again, or ever raise your voice to me, I'll show everyone what it looks like to get your ass kicked by a girl in heels."

Shay got to his feet and looked at all of us giving him side eye. "I get it, six against one. Nothing new. Wait until everyone hears about this!" He shook his head.

"Nobody cares about the rich white kids you're always trying to impress," Donny growled.

Shay, like me, Donny, Kara and Jade, was Black. But you'd never see him hanging around with any Black folks.

"I'll remember that, Donny." Shay shrugged while fixing his tie.

"Yeah, and we'll all remember this, Shay," I cut in.

"Whatever." Shay turned back toward his SUV. Bringing up Martin's music shop was such an unnecessary move.

"You okay?" I looked at Mel.

"I would have dropped his ass ten out of ten times." She let out a breath as we all walked away from the school.

"So what's the plan?" Mel turned around. "Were y'all gonna drink?"

"I mean, there technically is school tomorrow," I said. Schools generally put prom on a Thursday night so kids wouldn't get wasted afterward, and Friday was when we'd get our final report card.

"That doesn't mean we can't have a little fun . . ." Jade reached into her purse and grabbed a bottle.

"Oh em gee!" Azra was amazed. "You brought that to prom?"

"Of course." Jade laughed. "Prom is something to remember, right?" She took a swig. "Any takers?"

"I'm driving," Mel reminded her.

Kara grabbed the bottle and took a swig. "It's the shy ones who surprise us."

"I'll give it a try," I said.

"Pft," Mel scoffed. "You never even drank before!"

Donny laughed so hard he clutched his stomach.

"Thanks for that . . ." I shrugged as Kara passed me the bottle. Everyone watched me. It was weird. Their eyes locked on me like I was everyone's kid brother. I was the

19

shy kid. I didn't come out of my shell much. That was going to change. I was feeling brave that night.

So I took a large swig of the alcohol and felt my throat burn almost instantly. I managed to get most of it down, but I couldn't stop coughing.

"Whoa, slow down, AC." Mel put a hand on my shoulder while everyone laughed.

"That tastes like acid!" I gasped for air while Donny was cracking up.

Something did happen. I felt immediately at ease. Later I would learn it was the alcohol hitting my bloodstream, and I laughed just like everyone else.

★ ★ ★

We spent the rest of the night in the park. Kara and Azra sat on the swings, Donny sat on top of the jungle gym next to Jade and I was lying in the grass with Mel.

"How you feeling?" Mel giggled.

"Fine." I had the dumbest grin on my face. That night I found out I was a lightweight, and I felt real safe with the company I was with.

"Did you have a good birthday?" I asked.

"Yes," Mel said without a second thought. "I'm with the people I love, in some random park, everyone is dressed up and there's a full moon above our heads. The surprise may not have worked, but you still gave me a memory, so stay still." Mel reached into her purse to grab her Polaroid camera. She put it in position and snapped a shot.

"Not much is better than right now," I said as the photo popped out with a whirr.

"It's going to be nicer when I'm outside the city with these babes. We're gonna kick ass at Battle of the Bands. We'll win that tour money and make a real name for ourselves," she said while shaking the photo. That was Mel's plan, and she was intent on sticking to it. I wish I could make up my mind that easily.

"Yeah . . ." I replied. She handed me the photo to take a peek. Both of us smiling, my face a little drunk, and happy. I lowered it to see her looking directly at me.

"Your dad still after you about that business program?" Mel got straight to the point.

"It's the only thing he ever wants to talk about. He's like, 'You hear from CBU yet? We have to schedule a tour!'" I imitated. "It's like he forgot I'm wait-listed, and like that'll somehow change."

"Well, you know. That is a possibility," Mel shrugged.

"You too?" I mock-gasped.

"I'm just trying to be realistic." She took a breath. "Is that where you see yourself? Sitting in some cubicle? Running a business? Being a diehard capitalist?"

"Who says I don't wanna be a weekend warrior?" I shrugged, then Mel jokingly punched my arm.

"I'm kidding," I laughed. "No. Listen, I knew I'd be wait-listed in business admin. I just did it so Dad would get off my back."

"Yeah, well, that's the obvious part. I bet you knew you'd be wait-listed in community studies too," Mel said.

Like business admin, programs like community studies,

social services and child and youth studies, fill up quick. Part of me knew that's where I wanted to go, but another part of me wasn't ready to let go of everything.

"What stopped you?" she asked. "I know you." She gently stuck a finger in my chest. "I read what you wrote tonight. You're soft, gentle, a good listener with an honest heart. You're someone the world needs. Why did you wait so long?"

"I'm . . . scared, I guess." I sat up.

"Scared of what?" Mel sat up too.

"Adulthood, things changing." I gulped. "Losing all of this. Losing you."

I looked over as Mel's shoulders dropped.

"Mel, I never expected to get this scholarship. And I'm unsure if I wanna go to university yet," I confessed.

"That fear about losing each other is mutual." She gripped my hand. "You know I plan to hit the road with these girls after summer, regardless of if we win this Battle of the Bands contest. We'll figure it out. The last place you should be is a place where you're not committed. We got the space if you wanna come along."

The idea excited me. Was it selfish that I wanted to spend time with them just a little longer? One more year? We were still young, and we had the rest of our lives to figure all of this out.

"What do you suggest I do?" I asked.

"I think more than anything, you should be true to this." She pointed to my heart.

"What are y'all getting sentimental about over there?" Kara called to us from the swings.

"It sounds like you're trying to convince Adrian to come with us!" Azra yelled as Mel blushed.

"There shouldn't even need to be convincing. It's going to be bomb as hell!" Kara yelled back.

We both laughed. It would be bomb to spend time with them all on the road. There were a lot of things to get involved with, especially with that group. I knew no matter what happened, we'd be okay as long as we were all together.

"Don't spend your time waiting on a list, when you can come find a new place you haven't been." Mel rested a hand on my cheek.

I think that's when I knew my heart belonged with them. I liked the idea of sitting in my own driver's seat. I thought about what we could do in Montreal, Toronto and even Ottawa. We wouldn't have to worry about school, or anyone else's expectations.

"Okay," I replied with a stupid drunk grin.

Mel's face lit up, and she wrapped her arms around me. "We knew you would come around." She kept kissing my cheek as the photo fell onto the grass.

"Wait, have you guys been guessing when I might say yes?" I asked, realizing my face was now covered in lipstick.

"I honestly thought you'd say yes three weeks ago," Jade said from the jungle gym.

"I guessed somewhere this week!" Azra called over.

"We knew you would," Kara laughed.

The hard part would be telling my parents what my heart was set on. We didn't have to think about that on prom night. Instead we lay in a grass field, looking up at the few stars we could see, knowing we would be driving under more of them soon enough. Who wouldn't want to jump in a van and go on a great journey with the people they love most?

CHAPTER 2
Senior Year

I woke up the next morning feeling like my head had taken a beating. I fought my way out of bed and opened my laptop, hoping to read some comments from my new post. As the page refreshed, my phone started ringing.

"Hello?" I answered.

"Good morning, AC!" Mel's voice went right through my skull.

"Good morning," I sighed.

"Aw, does the baby have a hangover?" That made me grin, even if it was annoying. "I was calling to see if you were still up for tonight?"

"Yeah, yeah. Tonight. Meet you at the waterfront for seven?"

"You know the spot. The real question is, can you make it to class?" she asked, as I heard a notification. I switched tabs on my laptop, thinking one of the teens replied. No one did. I switched tabs again to my email, and there was something new. The subject line read: "Cape Breton University Admissions update."

My heart instantly sank into my stomach.

"Uh . . . Yeah. Gotta go. See you at school. Love you." I hung up and started breathing heavily.

After trying and failing to slow my heart rate down, I opened the email.

Dear Adrian Carter,

On behalf of Cape Breton University's admissions office, it is our pleasure to inform you there is an opening in our Business Administration Program for the Fall Semester. Your application has been selected with careful consideration based on your academic achievements. We are pleased to welcome you to Cape Breton University's School of Business. This email is time sensitive. Please contact us within a week's time to confirm your enrollment.

Sincerely,

Cape Breton University Admissions

"This is bad."

"Good morning, good morning!" Dad barged into my room as I shut my laptop.

"Dad!" I spun around. "What's up? I thought you would have left for work by now?"

"I decided to take the day off." He took a sip of coffee. "Gotta catch up on spring cleaning."

"Wait, why? You never take any time off!" I was confused.

"Well, I thought today would be different. Besides, it's your last day of school, so we're getting breakfast." He smiled and sat on my bed. "And you get to decide."

★ ★ ★

"Out of all the places we could have gone to breakfast, you choose McDonald's?" Dad shook his head as we sat in an empty parking lot.

"You have no idea how good this tastes right now." I bit into a breakfast sandwich.

"Ha, don't worry. I get it. It's to soothe that little hangover you got." Dad poked my head.

"Hangover?" I tensed up. "What are you talking about?"

"C'mon, you thought I didn't hear you stumbling up the steps when you got home at three a.m. last night?"

I got caught.

"Don't worry, I won't tell your mother. Besides, it isn't like you're not gonna be doing those things in university." His words sent a shiver up my spine. "I still have hope y'know. People drop out all the time during the summer leading up. You still have a big chance, and that scholarship won't go to waste."

"Yeah . . ." I sighed. Dad wanted this really bad for me, even if I didn't. Was it selfish that I didn't want to just get up and leave yet?

"Did you hear I'm working at the library again this summer?" I tried to change topics.

"Yeah, your mother told me. Don't spend all your money though, a scholarship only does so much. You have to

27

think about textbooks, supplies and groceries, too." He put the car in drive.

"Right." I sighed at him not taking the hint.

When Dad pulled up to the school, he put the car in park and turned to me.

"Listen, I know there's going to be parties and wild things to get into. I want you to have fun, but I just need you to promise me you'll stay focused." Dad placed a hand on my shoulder. "You have no idea how lucky you are. You're graduating with honours, and won a scholarship. Can you at least smile about it?" he joked while sitting back in the driver's seat.

"Who knows if I'll even get to use it?" I shrugged, hoping the moment would pass.

"You will. I'm just glad you have your head screwed on better than I did at your age."

"Hard to believe that," I shot back. "Growing up you had catchphrases like 'hard work sees results.' 'Study now and watch it pay off later.' 'Never let potential go to waste,'" I mimicked.

Dad shook his head and laughed. "That type of work ethic doesn't come naturally to everyone. It didn't come naturally to me." He shifted uncomfortably and let out a breath. "I had great grades at one point. I was a shoo-in for some universities, but instead of focusing on school, I was more focused on being popular and hitting up all the parties I could. I was so focused on making memories that I never focused on what mattered: setting up a solid future.

"I . . . uh . . ." He paused. "Because of my shortcomings at the time, I lost a scholarship for the University of Ottawa."

Dad had never mentioned any of this before. I almost couldn't believe it, considering how hard he was pushing for me to go to university. Maybe that was why? "You have no idea what I would do to be in your shoes." A smile broke through his regret as he patted my shoulder. "A, I know I'm not always the easiest to read, but I'm proud of you. So is your mother. You have a good head on your shoulders. You're young, gifted and I know wherever you go, you'll be doing good work."

"Thanks, Dad," I said in a low voice. I knew the conversation about taking time off from school to travel would be so much harder now, so I took a breath, preparing to get it out of the way, anyway. "Can I tell you someth —"

The passenger door flew open. "Good morning, Mr. Carter!" I looked up to see Mel. "I'm hijacking your son!" She pulled me from the car.

"Good morning to you too, Mel," Dad laughed. "How are things going with your band?"

"We're kicking ass, ruining boys' lives. Not this one though." She dusted off my shoulder.

"Well I'm thankful for that. You two have fun tonight, and stay safe!"

"Always. I'll bring him back before his bedtime," she said, as I blushed.

Dad drove off while Mel and I walked toward the school.

"So get this, Azra told me Ms. Phillips plans to give us some elite graduate pins at the end of the day like some badge of honour. I plan to make mine fish food tonight," Mel said, but I was still processing what Dad told me. That was the second time he ever said he was proud of me. The first was —

"Earth to Adrian?" Mel waved her hand in my face. "Plan on telling me why you hung up earlier? That hangover more than you expected?"

"Sorry, I —"

"Quick, I have to show you guys something!" Donny popped up, wrapping his arms around us and rushing to the other side of the parking lot. We watched the school bus make its way to the curb. As the door opened, an unimpressed Shay Smith stepped out.

"Hey, Shay!" Donny called as loud as he could. "Nice new wheels!"

Other students around the entrance looked toward Shay. Some of them snickered and others whispered.

"Donny, that's cold." I laughed.

"It's how revenge is best served." Mel grinned.

"That's what he gets for making me to go to Bayers Lake later," Donny said as Shay walked up to us.

"Is there a problem?" Shay approached with an angry look on his face.

"Problem?" I looked from side to side. "I'm actually proud of you for cutting down on your eco footprint."

"Trucks aren't great for that," Mel added matter-of-factly.

"Funny. Just so you know, this isn't over." Shay stalked away, fuming as we giggled. The bell rang, and Mel turned to me. "I gotta head to class. Let's talk later, okay?"

"Okay," I replied as she left.

"I hope I didn't interrupt," Donny said. *Not that he cares.*

"Donny, you have no idea what happened this morning."

"Well, you have a free first period, and I'm skipping chem. Let's chat."

★ ★ ★

Donny and I chilled out in the cafeteria. He ate a chicken sandwich while I sat there, arms crossed.

"So, let me get this straight," he spoke with his mouth full. "You got an acceptance email from CBU, and you don't wanna tell your dad that this business program isn't your choice?"

"More or less," I groaned. "It's . . . if I tell him the truth about waiting for this community studies seat, he'll say it's stupid. It's a waste of time, and I should focus on just getting out into the world."

"He won't say that. He knows what you've been through, and the work you're doing in these groups."

"That's the thing, Donny." I looked around. "Dad never even knew I had a . . . you know."

"Wait, really?" Donny raised an eyebrow. "Why didn't you ever tell him?"

"C'mon, you know my dad. Macho man, MMA, football, baseball super fan. Imagine hearing that his son had . . ." I stared at the table, sighing, "an eating disorder."

"Damn, that's sad, man. I'm sorry," Donny said. "Then I imagine there's Mel. Have you told her about this CBU stuff?"

I didn't reply.

"Listen, bro. I don't know much about relationships,

but I know that's a conversation you need to have sooner than later."

He was right. We'd have to talk tonight.

I lifted my head. "I'll talk to her. We'll figure out a plan. We'll make it work."

"The day CBU sent me my acceptance email, they gave me a call as a reminder, so be sure to check your phone and don't make any decisions yet," Donny said. Donny had been accepted into sociology at the beginning of the year. Unlike me, he was excited for university. I'd imagine he wasn't too sad to know I was accepted too.

"Good to know."

The last day was really anything besides productive. We spent most of the day either watching movies or posting group photos on Instagram. I didn't hear from Mel at lunch, so I chilled in the library, and we watched TV.

Not the last class of the day though: African Canadian Literature. I sat with university applications on my desk like every other student in the room. Mr. Price was going on with the same speech he had been all year. "Apply for the scholarships that are still left. There's always a higher chance of receiving them than you think." Mr. Price stood up from his desk. "Look at Josh who received a Dal scholarship a few months back, and Tasha who got into SMU, first year free of charge." He smiled at the two students. Black lit always felt like our homeroom. Mr. Price took care of us, and honestly just let us be us. With that being said, he didn't let us be lazy. He always wanted us ready for the world.

My phone vibrated in my pocket.

It had to be CBU. I ignored it.

"Shay and Adrian were both awarded our Citadel Phoenix Scholarship, for academic success, exemplifying leadership and unparalleled growth." Mr. Price looked over at me. "It's the first of its kind, and if these two keep up their grades, we'll be committed to supporting up to half of their academic careers."

"I think it involves character." Shay looked at me. "You can't pretend to love working with kids one day and be complicit with destroying someone else's property the next."

"Real subtle, Mr. For the People yet turns into a cry-baby when someone parks in his spot," I shot back.

"All right, bring it back." Mr. Price tried getting me and Shay to calm down. "I'm just saying you two have a lot to be proud of here. From reaching academic success to receiving scholarships. For people like us, going to university is more than just representing yourself. You're also representing your community. This is a responsibility that you have to be ready to handle."

I suddenly felt so much pressure on my shoulders that I couldn't speak up. Carrying that kind of weight didn't exactly ease my anxiety. My heart was set on travelling with Mel, not representing an entire community.

The bell rang, cutting through Mr. Price's speech about life post-grad.

"And with that, I'll see you all dressed up at graduation," he said proudly. "I know what you all think. It's true, the pleasure was yours," he finished as we laughed. "Congratulations."

I snuck out of the room before they could celebrate, hoping to find a voicemail. When I checked my phone, there was a voicemail, but not from CBU, it was from . . . "Dad?"

I opened it immediately.

"Adrian, it's Dad! Listen, you just got a call from Cape Breton University. What did I tell you? They offered you a seat to start in September. We have to sign up for one of their tours to get you ready this summer! Call me when you can."

"This isn't good," I said as the message ended. I must have put my home phone on the application. I banged my head on a locker. "Stupid. Stupid. Stupid." There was no way I could go home.

So instead, I went to Redemption House Cafe a couple blocks from the school. I opened up my laptop and saw there were some notifications from the ED support group. The first read:

"Wow, thank you for sharing your story."

Another:

"It's good to see we're not alone."

I was glad I could make others feel comfortable, even if in that moment I was struggling. I began reading some of their intro posts, about who they were, what schools they went to, their insecurities. It wasn't that different from what I'd gone through, being bullied over my appearance, feeling eyes staring at me. I remember after I lost weight how different people treated me. That was the worst part.

I remember how different Dad treated me. It was the first time he told me he was proud of me, and that morning was the second. I loved my dad, but resented that he didn't know what I went through, or the toll it took on me. It felt like he was only proud of the things I'd done, instead of who I was. I knew he believed in hard work, but sometimes I just wished he believed in me. I always thought maybe he was ashamed of me for being bigger, and I was too afraid of what the answer might be to bring it up. I just wished I didn't have to prove myself to feel appreciated by my dad.

"Adrian?" I looked up to see Azra standing at my table.

"Azra? What's up?" I shut my laptop. I hadn't expected to see her.

"Not much." She took a seat. "I seen you in the window, and wondered if you had a minute."

"Always. How's it going?"

Azra and Mel were pretty close. They met in the elite class and were the only two people of colour there. Mel's grandparents on her mom's side were from India, and Azra was from Syria. People at punk shows always looked at Azra funny for wearing a hijab, but she showed every time that she could rock with the best drummers around. You don't have to be a certain way to be great.

"Man, I'm glad school is over and we can focus on this Battle of the Bands business." She let out a breath. "First show is tomorrow night, and I was gonna go over a setlist with Mel after school."

"Oh? Why aren't you with her?"

"I was hoping you might know. I think she bailed sometime during lunch. It doesn't sound like her."

Azra was right. It didn't sound like Mel. Especially after she made sure I was going to school that day.

"If you're meeting up with her later, give her this." Azra slid something across the table. I grabbed it and saw it was a pin engraved with 'EG'. Elite graduate.

"Will do." I looked up, and then sent Mel a text.

Me: Everything okay?

I didn't hear back, so in the meantime I sat with Azra and opted out of going home. She was much better company than the anxiety I buried deep in my stomach.

When Redemption House closed, I sent Mel another text.

Me: Hey, still meeting at the waterfront?
Mel: Make it the roof of the school.

I wondered why Mel wanted to change location. She spent most of her time throughout the last couple years taking care of the garden on the school's rooftop. It was a calming place for her. I wondered if her dad was on her back again. I knew Mel could handle him, even if he put the weight of the world on her shoulders.

Once I got to the school, I found the fire escape and made my way up. I smelled cigarette smoke in the distance and saw Mel sitting on a blanket, her back turned to me.

"Hey . . . I thought you quit." I approached and sat, seeing a cigarette in her hand.

Mel exhaled smoke and looked at me awkwardly. Something must have been up.

"Can we talk?" We both spoke over each other.

"You go first," we both said at the same time again.

"What's up, Mel?" I asked. That's when I noticed her eyes were red. She had been crying.

"A lot . . ." she said. "Not the good a lot either. It's the stressful kind of a lot."

"Oh," I replied. Mel wasn't really one to let me see her cry often.

"What's wrong?" I asked.

"Everything, Adrian."

I looked at the ground behind her, and there was an envelope lying there.

"Is that the letter from your car?"

"Yeah." Mel picked it up.

"Where's it from?"

"A ghost story. That's where it's from." She handed it to me. It read:

To Melody,

There are so many ways I could start a letter to you. Firstly, I would like to say congratulations on everything. I hope this reaches you for your birthday. It seems more sincere than a text. I've been keeping up with you and telling everyone in Toronto about my daughter, my song, my Melody. Your father and I are speaking again, and I know you and him have issues. I know you and I have similar issues. I am hoping we can find common ground in the coming weeks, as I am making a trip to Halifax for your graduation.

I miss you dearly, love you infinitely and will see you soon.

— Mom

My heart dropped into my stomach.

"Mel, that's your mom," I said.

"Yeah, Adrian. I haven't seen my mom in years, and now she's just showing up out of the blue." She began getting teary-eyed.

Mel never told me the complete story about her mother. I guess I assumed she would tell me whenever she was ready. I knew in that moment she was really hurt, and I wish I knew what to say, or what to do, but I didn't, and that was the worst feeling in the world for me.

"She left me when I was a kid." Tears rolled down her cheeks. "After the divorce, one day, she just left. Vanished, and left me behind."

I pulled her into a hug. She rested her head on my shoulder. I could tell she was tired. Life was never an easy ride for her, and she never liked asking for help. I wanted her to know she wasn't alone.

"You never deserved that," I said.

"Well, it's what I got," she replied, holding onto my arm.

"So, she'll be here in a few days? If it's too hard, and you need a place to crash, I know me and my parents wouldn't mind."

"I know, and I'll probably take you up on that." Mel took a breath.

"Is the letter why you left school today?" I asked.

"How'd you know?"

"Azra gave me this." I handed her the pin.

Mel grabbed it, lifted her head and sat up, looking at the pin for a good minute. She closed her eyes and took a few more deep breaths.

I really wished the world wasn't the way it was, but there wasn't much I could do about it. In that moment, the only thing I knew how to do was to be there for her. It was exactly where I needed to be.

Mel finally opened her eyes and threw the pin off the rooftop to land in the fountain outside the school.

"I guess you already know how I feel about the elite class," Mel said, resting her head back on my shoulder. "The coming weeks are going to be a dumpster fire."

I guess that was one way to put it. I knew she was coming to terms with letting all of it go. School, the elite class and the city.

"You said you had something you wanted to talk about?" Mel looked up at me.

Right. CBU. The promise. Dad.

I felt hesitant to bring it up after the news from Mel. Maybe unloading everything that happened wasn't the best idea, not then, at least.

"What did you want to say?" she asked again.

"I, uh . . ." I didn't even know what I was trying to say. "I really . . . like . . ."

"You really like what?" She raised an eyebrow.

I'm probably the worst at being fly under pressure, and I didn't see an easy way out of this conversation without me making an idiot of myself, so I continued to dig my own grave by saying, ". . . pineapple on pizza . . ."

Mel was left expressionless. "Really?"

"Yeah, like a lot."

"No, you don't."

"Yes, I do."

"No, you don — Listen, whatever it is, tell me when you're ready. I kinda have a lot going on right now."

"Okay," I replied. She knew it was something. I just couldn't bring myself to talk about it. Not then. She had the weight of everything else on her shoulders. I couldn't bear to add any more to the baggage.

CHAPTER 3

Brown, Black & Infamous

I decided to spend the night at Mel's and avoid home. I told Dad she needed me, and he understood. My parents had probably called all our distant relatives to tell them the big news that I was in university, just like they did after I lost weight. I was glad to get away, so much that I didn't bother going home the next day. Meaning I had to help the band set up for their show at Dreamer's Corner.

"Adrian, take the amp," Azra said from behind me. I turned toward the band's van. It belonged to Kara. She bought it two summers ago, but it wasn't until last year that she dedicated the entire van to the band. It was painted brown and black, with Brown, Black & Infamous written on both sides. It got the word out. That was for sure. Heck, last summer they had hit up music festivals from Yarmouth all the way up to Cape Breton on a provincial tour. I didn't go along, but when they returned, Mel told me we had to drive up to the Cabot Trail during the Fall. I had never been up there, but I'm sure I'd see it sooner or later.

"Hurry up, Adrian!" Azra dropped the amp in my arms.

"Uh oh." I caught hold of it. "I got it!"

I heard the back door of the venue open, and I could hear Kara's voice.

"What's taking y'all so long?"

"Adrian is over here daydreaming again," Azra sighed.

"Figures."

"I'm coming, I'm coming," I said, carrying the amp up the steps inside. The backstage was pretty empty, besides Jade and Mel going over the set list.

"So, we start off with 'Codeswitch' and end with 'The Movement.'" Mel looked up at Jade.

"Yeah, yeah, how do you feel about it?" Jade sounded excited.

Mel smiled. "We're gonna kill it."

Mel was super focused that day, and I tried to give her some space before the show. Even if I was still worried about her after the night before.

"Adrian?" Mel turned and looked at me. "You have the amp, cool." She took it from me. "We gotta get started on sound check."

"Where's the other band?" I asked Jade as she took her bass out of the case.

"Those fake punks? Ugh, they have a history of being late." Jade shook her head.

"They might wanna hurry." I shrugged.

"Why?" Kara asked, walking into the room with Azra,

both carrying pieces of the drum set. "They'll have a team doing the sound check for them. Meanwhile, we gotta show up early, put in twice the amount of work and only get half the praise as those white boys." Kara continued walking past me.

"Oh," I replied, feeling silly for even mentioning it. Kara was right, punk seemed pretty male dominated, and you didn't see too many people who looked like . . . us.

The place began to fill up while I stood against the wall waiting for Donny near the main floor. As everyone began arriving, I started to feel uncomfortable. Not that I didn't like the music, but folks were staring at me as if I wasn't supposed to be there. Years ago, when Mel took me to my first show, I remember some dude kept asking if I was "the guy." I think he thought I was a drug dealer. Now I was a scholarship kid, and they still gave me those same looks.

Donny gave me a gentle punch on the arm as he arrived. "They giving you those looks again?"

I snorted. "As usual."

"I can't wait to get out of this city," Donny said, annoyed.

"You act like Cape Breton will be any better," I laughed.

"And you act like five people of colour driving across the country in a van will be a vacation." He smirked. I didn't laugh.

That's when we overheard some dude talking way too loudly. "Spartan of The Suns are going to smoke these girls."

"You sure about that?" Donny said without even looking in his direction. Five suburban-looking dude bros turned our way.

"Uh, duh. We played with them last summer at Punk Fest," the bro said.

"And who the hell are you?" Donny poked the bear. "Generic bro one? With generic bro two, and generic bro three and four? I think that'd be a great idea for shirt, though you'll owe me fifteen per cent of sales."

"I'm Chet." He looked offended that Donny even asked. "I'm the lead singer of 3AM." He pointed to his chest.

Donny started giggling, and I did too. 3AM was a notorious band of punks from the west end of Halifax. They were entitled, rich and out of touch. 3AM was known for trashing venues. They had a large following on social media, mostly because they had loads of money for promo.

"What's so funny?" Chet raised an eyebrow. The other three were visibly upset.

"Of course, that's the name of your band." Donny laughed as loud as he could, and I did too. Everyone looked over. Chet's face turned red as he stalked to the back and slammed a door.

Our laughter faded when a man in overalls and a beanie jumped on stage, yelling, "All right, Halifax, who's ready for your first round of the Maritime Indie Battle of the Bands Tournament!"

The crowd erupted so loud that it stung my ears. I covered them as I watched white dudes take over the stage and pick up their guitars. The lead singer was already screaming in the mic before the others were ready.

Donny and I stood to the side, not giving the band

much of a reaction. We had to save our energy for Mel. With that being said, Spartans of The Sun sucked. The guitarist's amp made an obnoxious buzzing sound, and the lead singer tried to scream over it. Donny and I covered our ears until two bouncers, one tall, one short, came up to us.

"Hey, you causing trouble?" the tall bouncer asked. He was a bald white guy who looked like he could snap us in half. "Answer me, boy," he said when Donny shrugged.

"Who are you calling boy?" I asked. "We're just hanging out."

"Yeah, right." The short bouncer snorted. "You in on it too?"

"In on what?" I asked.

"Harassing bands, stealing posters from the merch table."

"Stolen posters?" Donny was confused. "I can't tell if it's the steroids or protein shakes that got to your head. What makes you think we stole anything?"

"Don't be stupid," the bald one said.

"Don't be racist," Donny replied, causing their faces to turn red.

The tall man grabbed Donny's arm, twisting it. I tried to stop him, but the other one came from behind and grabbed my arms. They dragged us to the back, shoved us both into a room and slammed the door.

"What the hell are you doing?" Donny tried to shove the bouncer, and was met with a push that made him hit the table.

"Here's what I want, you two, empty your pockets, and give that band their merch back!" the tall one hollered.

Okay, I was terrified. I looked over at Donny, and he nodded at me. We both emptied our pockets. All I had was a wallet, house keys and my cell phone. Donny had just about the same.

The two bouncers looked at each other, both confused, as if they expected more.

"Is this what you want? A couple of fucking house keys and cell phones? You think we could fit posters in our pockets, dumbass?" Donny yelled. He was a lot braver than I was.

"You said it was a Black guy who stole the posters." The tall man looked at his partner who just shrugged. "I'll get that girl from the band."

So they went after the only two Black guys at the entire show? I had no idea who was stealing posters. After a few minutes of getting hard side eye from the shorter one, I heard footsteps followed by a trustworthy voice.

"What the *fuck*!" I looked up to see Kara. "What do you think you're doing with my friends?"

The tall guy's entire bald head turned red. Not from being mad, from the embarrassment.

"Did you just profile the only two Black guys at this show? Because I got low patience for this bullshit. A poster is a poster, but you dragging them in here isn't even hiding your racism!" Kara went off. "Guys, get back out there. I have some words for this asshole." She pointed at the tall guy, who seemed to be in charge.

"Listen, I'm sorry about what happened," the short bouncer apologized as he walked us out of the room and led us to a table. "Honestly. Free meal on the house."

Donny looked over at me with a grin.

"Your walkie-talkie there?" Donny pointed to the radio on the bouncer's belt.

"It's a radio," he corrected.

"Okay. So, your walkie-talkie there? Can you order to the kitchen?"

"I guess so." He shrugged.

"Well, order us reparation nachos," Donny said with a straight face while I completely lost myself in laughter.

The young bouncer's face lost all of its colour and he responded with, "Come on, man —"

"Do it or this will be on the news tomorrow. If you didn't know, I'm Brown, Black & Infamous's PR coordinator," Donny lied while staring into the man's soul. It was an open secret that Dreamer's Corner couldn't use any more bad press after the news broke out about them underpaying staff a few months back.

The security guard grabbed his radio and made a defeated face. "I would like to order . . ." he sighed. "Reparation nachos."

Donny and I laughed our asses off when the food came and looked over the dance floor.

"Reparation nachos? Really?" I howled while Donny tried to catch his breath.

"We gotta have our fun everyone once in a while. Knowing this space isn't exactly . . . for us." Donny looked off into the crowd.

He was right. I looked around and saw nobody who looked like us. We were easily seen as different. I really hoped Kara didn't tell Mel what happened. I wouldn't want her to lose focus.

"So . . ." Donny trailed off. "You're not seriously gonna throw away that scholarship for this, are you?" Donny asked.

"Donny . . ." I looked up.

"Do you really wanna be accused of this shit all the time? Always being treated like you don't belong? Do you know what I'd do for a scholarship like yours? Like Shay's? I'm already in CBU but you guys are ahead of the curve," he reasoned. "Don't you think your dad just wants the best for you? So you don't have to deal with stuff like this? Come on, man. Mr. Price said you represent the best of us, don't just throw it away."

I sat with that for a minute, and didn't answer him. I wasn't throwing away a scholarship for this. I just didn't want to say goodbye to Mel. Why did everyone else have to come into consideration when I decide my future?

"These nachos taste like gentrification," Donny said condescendingly while looking over at the kitchen staff. "Consider them a graduation gift. I'm outta here." Donny fixed his collar and walked off.

Damn. I put my head face down on the dirty table, then looked at the plate. Food was always complicated, and it was like the nachos were speaking to me, even if my heart told me to ignore them. I'd already had fast food the morning before. My stomach growled, realizing that was the last time I actually ate anything. I checked my phone to see the text I ignored.

Dad: Adrian, where have you been? We seriously need to talk.

I couldn't think about that right now. I drowned my grief with a nacho, and another, and another. I dug into that bowl of nachos faster than I should have, hoping it would smother the stress.

I don't even know how much time had passed. When I went to reach again, the bowl was empty.

"I shouldn't have done that." I put my head down again, then I heard Mel's voice over the guilt I felt.

"Now, there's about twice as many feet than there are bodies in here. I better see you moving, and that goes for you too, Adrian!"

I looked up to see Mel smiling at me from the stage as she gripped her guitar. A part of the audience laughed while looking over to me. I made my way to the dance floor and felt those nachos in my stomach.

"We're Brown, Black & Infamous!" Mel's voice echoed through the microphone as Jade started strumming a bass line that Azra followed up shortly on the drums. Kara finally brought in a guitar riff that led to Mel's voice flowing through the entire venue.

Mel rocked her hair back and forth while screaming lyrics to the crowd.

I looked up and caught eyes with Mel while Kara was in the middle of her solo. Mel stepped to the microphone and began screaming her lyrics again.

"Melanate the spaces! Stop pretending it's a pipe dream!"

The crowd erupted so loud it made me jump in the air. The sound was crisp, and a lot smoother than the other guys. I got lost somewhere in it. The thing about being in the middle of a crowd is that it gives you the opportunity to leave anxiety at the door. Somewhere in that moment of chaos, I let go of all the things the world wanted me to be, and just existed in a space where my shoulders weren't mountaintops of expectations. I didn't have to carry the responsibility Mr. Price talked about, or the guilt I felt about avoiding my father. I felt like I was in control.

It was like the entire bar was vibrating and I could barely keep my footing. Mel's giggling could be heard from the mic while the man in the overalls from earlier tried to speak over the crowd.

"All right, all right, can we get some noise for Spartans of The Sun!"

I stayed silent, feeling my heart beat while being surrounded by noise. There were a lot of people cheering from the sides, and I was hoping everyone in the middle could propel ourselves to be even louder.

"Okay, okay, let's make some noise for Brown, Black & Infamous!"

I yelled as loud as I could while the dance floor vibrated beneath my feet. It was like the entire room was shaking.

"Brown, Black & Infamous advances to round two!" the man in overalls yelled.

I grinned something stupid watching Mel, Kara, Jade and Azra celebrating on stage while Spartans of The Sun looked shook.

★ ★ ★

"We did it!" Mel laughed and pulled my hand as we walked under the night sky, back toward the North End.

"Did you see their faces? Like they couldn't believe they lost? That made my night!"

I was glad to see Mel so happy. Maybe the next week wouldn't be so bad. I guessed Kara never told her what happened.

"I'm not even mad someone stole our posters," she said as we entered a park called the Pit.

"Donny and I got hassled over that," I confessed.

"Really?" Mel froze and looked over at me. "Holy shit, Adrian. Are you okay?"

"Yeah, I'm fine," I sighed.

"No, you're not." Mel saw my arm. "This bruise. Did they put their hands on you?"

"I'm fine. Kara gave it to the bouncers." I put my arm around her.

"As she always does." I could still hear her disappointment. We walked toward an empty swing set at the bottom of the hill, and before she got on, Mel asked, "Why didn't you tell me?"

"I didn't wanna distract you."

She shoved my arm away.

"You're not a distraction, jerk," she said, grabbing a swing. "I'm not gonna stand for some 'roid rage losers putting their hands on my boyfriend."

I should have told her. I should have told her about the university news too. Even if I wasn't sure about it, I had to be transparent. Maybe we could get away from the stress and just talk about it.

"I know, I'm sorry."

"You're not the one who needs to apologize, Adrian."

She sounded conflicted.

We sat in silence for a moment, letting the air from the Pit calm us down. With round one out of the way, I thought it was time we probably talk. Though maybe a change in scenery would be good.

"Hey . . . Do you wanna get out of here? Go for a drive or something?" I tried to take attention away from the show. She looked at me and raised an eyebrow.

"Sounds like you just wanna find a makeout spot."

"What! I . . ." I blushed. "No . . . I mean . . . Maybe? But that's not what I meant."

"Then what do you mean?" She dug her feet into the rocks below the swing.

I knew the news about her mom still had to be bugging her, even if she didn't want to say it out loud. I just wish she didn't have to pretend otherwise.

"I wish you didn't always have to be the strong one," I told her. "I know you're going through a lot at home right now, and I don't want you to worry about me on top of that." I opened up as she turned around in her swing. "You always focus on being strong, but that doesn't mean you don't need softness, kindness or love either. You don't always have to do this part alone."

Our eyes met, and she gave me a surprised look, like she wasn't expecting that from me. She took my hand from her swing, and pulled herself over, landing a kiss on my cheek.

"I'm grateful for you, dork." She loosened her grip. We looked up at the stars above our heads. They were few and far between past the MacKay bridge.

"I'm sorry you had to deal with those racist idiots at the show."

"This wasn't the only time," I blurted, then kind of wished I hadn't. Mel and the band dealt with a lot of issues at the shows, but that didn't mean I hadn't either. I'm still a Black man, and seen as hyper-visible in a space where organizers love to treat women of colour, like Mel and her band, as invisible. Our experiences weren't exactly the same, but close enough to understand each other.

"Hey, listen, yesterday I got —" I started to say.

"I promise you," she cut me off, "nothing like that will happen to you again. We'll figure it out. We'll be better off once we're out of here. I want us to get lost in Montreal, experience downtown Toronto and visit some museums in Ottawa. More importantly, I want you to be safe," she told me as my phone began vibrating in my pocket. Before I could see who it was, she grabbed my hand again. "We're gonna get a Wi-fi adapter installed in Kara's van. You can keep doing your advocacy online. That's important to you, so it's important to me too. We're getting more followers online that might help boost your work, and by the time we're back, I'm sure you'll have been accepted into community studies . . ."

I could still feel my phone vibrating, but I knew better than to answer it because I knew it was Dad.

"We don't have to stay in this city where people like us don't get a fair shot. We can ditch it, find a place worth going. I promise you it'll be worth it," Mel said.

I ignored Dad because Mel wanted me there. Was it wrong that I wanted to be there too?

CHAPTER 4

Graduation

"We did it!" Donny celebrated way too loud. "We got honours, man!"

"Shh," I cut him off. "Principal Cook is speaking." Donny and I sat in a crowd of students, all wearing blue gowns with the ridiculous hats. I felt silly. Donny, on the other hand, loved every moment of it. He also loved ignoring our principal just as much.

Graduation took place in the Halifax Forum, where they usually held hockey games. Halifax West held their graduation in the morning, meaning Citadel had the afternoon. All the students sat in plastic chairs where the rink would be, split into two sides with a black carpet in between that led to the stage. I knew my parents were somewhere in the crowd above. Dad really wasn't impressed I'd been avoiding him. I spent the night at Mel's after the show and spent Sunday night at Donny's when I started getting Facebook messages from cousins, aunts, uncles and my grandparents. Of course Dad told everyone. I woke up early to run home, grab a pair of clothes and dart out of the house before either of my parents woke up.

"Whatever. Mr. Cook is trash. He told me in grade ten I'd be lucky to even see a mark over sixty, and here I am with honours!"

"Donny King," Mr. Cook called over the microphone. "I need your attention for thirty more minutes, then you never have to see me again."

Subtle laughter lit up parts of the forum, myself included. That man was happy to see Donny leave, but at least Donny proved him wrong.

Mr. Cook readjusted himself and continued, "Tomorrow, you embark on the first day of the future. It's been both an honour and privilege to be the principal of Citadel High. I'm proud to introduce the valedictorian, Shay Smith."

"Here we go." I rolled my eyes.

"Good afternoon, Citadel." Shay walked up to the microphone with a smile and students applauded. Donny and I didn't say anything. I looked over to see Kara shake her head while Jade was texting on her phone. I couldn't find Mel though I knew she was there. I also knew her mom was there too. She got in last night, and when I sent Mel a text that morning, she never replied. I was so nervous about it that I forgot the . . .

"Shit, I forgot the flowers," I whispered.

Donny convinced me it would be a good idea to buy Mel flowers, and to give them to her right in front of her mother so I could make a great first impression. I wasn't that sentimental, but Donny insisted it was a good idea. Maybe it was, considering I was already on Martin's bad side.

"Today we reflect upon the years we spent in these class-rooms and hallways, and the amount of knowledge we were privileged enough to gain," Shay spoke over my thoughts.

"I put the flowers in my backseat," Donny said. "You forgot them when you left this morning."

"You're a lifesaver." I let out a breath as Donny handed me his keys.

After the rest of Shay's dry speech, the principal finally started calling names of the graduates. I sat there watching him give students handshakes and whispering something to them while handing out diplomas. It was weird. I actually felt excited once they got to the C surnames.

"You're coming up, bro!" Donny cheered.

When the principal called "Adrian Carter" a good chunk of the school erupted. Donny put a hand on my shoulder and yelled, "Go get it, bro!"

I got up from my seat and walked toward the stage thinking, *Please don't trip, please don't trip, please don't trip.*

Luckily I didn't. When I walked onto the stage, it got loud. It felt bittersweet at best. Three years ago, I was just the fat kid. The one people snickered at in the halls, the butt of the joke, the pity party. I was treated different for who I was. They didn't see me that way anymore. But it didn't mean they saw me as the mentor, or eating disorder recovery advocate I was aiming to be. They only saw me as worthy because I was the fat kid who lost weight.

"Adrian Carter is the recipient of our Citadel Phoenix Scholarship," Mr. Cook said as I walked across to meet him. He shook my hand and passed me my diploma with the other.

"I bet you couldn't have imagined that three years ago, huh? We're all proud of your success, Adrian. We know you're going to have a bright future." He smiled at me.

"Thank you, sir." I took a breath. I looked to my left and on the far side of the Forum I could see Mel smiling with Azra. Mel was the only person who never treated me different after my weight loss, because I think she was the only one who understood. And because of that, she was the only one who ever made me feel safe talking about it. I rushed outside with those thoughts to find Donny's ride and grab the bouquet of flowers in the backseat. As I grabbed them, my phone vibrated. It was a text from Mom.

Mom: Where'd you go? Your father and I have a surprise.

Ugh. I didn't think I could handle any more surprises. At least I knew they were looking for me, so I snuck back in and stayed close to the stage, watching my friends make their walk. When Donny walked by Mr. Cook, he pretended to give him a handshake but instead swiped his hand away, combing his hair. Donny's level of petty was untouchable.

Eventually I heard, "Congratulations, Melody Woods!" Mr. Cook's voice echoed through the entire room while the remaining folks cheered. I rushed to the opposite side of the stage and watched her wave to the crowd of students and throw her hat into the air while laughing. She walked down to the steps and then she made her way offstage. I jumped from behind the curtains and half startled her.

"Adrian —" she said as I cut her off with a kiss. She held on for a minute.

"Okay, maybe you can surprise me every once in a while." She blushed, holding her diploma.

"I got you these." I pulled the bouquet from behind my back.

"Ha, flowers?" She was surprised, stepping into me and grabbing hold of them.

"Yeah, I kinda feel like being super sappy today." I grinned.

"I can see that. You know you didn't have to —"

"I wanted to," I reassured her.

She gave me a hug, then pulled my hand as she walked toward the entrance.

There were so many graduates taking pictures with their parents as Mel led me along. I could barely see a thing. It was like we were in a wave of blue gowns until I heard Martin's voice.

"Melody! Over here!"

Mel pulled me through a small crowd, and I almost tripped. When I looked up, I saw an unfamiliar woman give Mel a hug. Mel didn't hug back; she just soaked it in.

"I'm so proud of you!" The woman squeezed Mel while closing her eyes, and when she opened them, they met mine. It was like I was looking at Mel's clone, and it was weirder than it sounds.

She gasped with excitement. "You must be . . ."

"Mom . . . stop," Mel said as she let her go.

"You're Adrian?" The woman approached me.

". . . Yeah. I'm Adrian . . ." I stuttered and extended my hand.

"It's nice to finally meet you!" She pulled me into a hug. "I'm Prisha, Melody's mother." Mel's mother was tall, and almost a spitting image of Mel. Long hair, dark skin and warm brown eyes.

"Hi, Prisha." I awkwardly hugged her back. The hug felt like an eternity.

"From what I hear, you sound like a very special young man." She let go and dusted off my shoulders. "The flowers were a nice touch." She smiled and squeezed my cheeks.

"Mom, could you not?" Mel took Prisha's hand away from my now-aching cheek.

"I'm sorry, just excited to meet him. And I'm even more excited to have dinner with him and his parents."

"Wait, what?" *When was this discussed?*

"That was our surprise." I heard Mom's voice from behind me. "Prisha called me this morning."

"Yeah. Right after you rushed out of the house after being away all weekend." Dad gave me side eye while handing me a garment bag with a blazer inside.

★ ★ ★

Later that evening, I had that same stunned look on my face while dressed up in a suit, tie and everything. I glanced across the table. Mel looked just as awkward as I was. We decided to go to a sushi restaurant.

Mel sat in between Martin and Prisha, while I sat in between my parents. Dad gave up on chopsticks and used a fork. It was as embarrassing as it sounded. I didn't know what to say, so I just played with a bowl of noodles while Mel stayed mute. Eventually, Prisha broke the silence.

"So . . . you must be very proud of your son, graduating with quite the scholarship."

"Yeah, he's our boy." Mom rested a hand on my shoulder. "He got some big news last week."

Mel raised an eyebrow when she heard that.

"I wouldn't have gotten any scholarship without Mel's help!" I cut Mom off before she mentioned CBU.

I couldn't let Mel find out from anyone but me. That would be bad, really bad. She looked up from the soup she had barely touched and just said, "You can take some credit too, y'know?"

"You graduated with honours too." I smiled nervously. "All while being in a band." I switched topics. Mel looked at me like she wanted to kill me for even bringing it up.

"Yes, I've heard a lot about that," Prisha said.

"They definitely make the house shake during practice," Martin sighed, then ate a mouthful of sushi.

"Yeah, Dad . . . It's almost like we're a rock band," Mel replied.

Prisha put a hand on Mel's back. I could see her instantly tense up. "Ever think about what you really want to do in the future? Something sustainable? Something to build upon?"

"I wanna build with these girls." Mel moved Prisha's hand away.

"Maybe after this competition business is over, you can apply to university." Martin took another bite.

"Dad!" Mel was annoyed. "I'm not applying to anything."

"What about you, Adrian?" Prisha looked directly at me. "What's your plan with this scholarship? Dal? SMU? Mount Saint Vincent?"

I could feel my arms tense as soon as Prisha asked me. Sitting between my parents made the situation even worse.

"Go ahead and tell them." Dad patted my shoulder.

Mel's gaze shot to me. "Tell us what?"

"It's nothing." I tried to play it off.

"Making it into business administration is nothing?" Dad looked confused.

My face turned red, and my jaw clenched instantly. It was like everything froze as I caught eyes with Mel. She looked at me in a way I wish didn't hurt so much.

"Adrian . . ." her voice was rocky. "When were you going to tell me this?"

My dad's face went from excited to cringe. Prisha's eyes widened and Mom frowned at me.

"CBU? Adrian, good for you, young man." Martin smiled. I couldn't tell if he was genuinely interested or not clued in.

Mel stood up, grabbed her coat and left. It didn't take long for me to get up from my seat, but Mom stopped me.

"Adrian!" She grabbed my hand. "You didn't tell her?"

"I know, I know." I stood up and ran after Mel.

CHAPTER 5
The Summer Between Us

I knew Mel had to be on the rooftop of the school. It was our spot. I ran up to the fire escape, feeling too sweaty for my blazer, and began climbing up. I had hoped to catch her somewhere along Spring Garden Road, but she was a lot faster than me.

When I got to the roof, I could see smoke in the distance. She didn't even turn to me before she asked, "Do you remember when we spoke about communication, and what that meant? And how you would be a better communicator, and you would be accountable, and blah, blah, blah."

"It wasn't all blah, blah, blah." I sighed and sat next to her, trying to catch my breath and loosening my tie.

"But you don't seem to be trying either." Mel looked at me. I could see her mascara staining her cheeks. "When were you going to tell me you got accepted?"

"I was going to tell you when things weren't so heavy."

"Ha! So never?" Mel shook her head, then took a puff. "Why didn't you think I could handle it?"

"It's not that you couldn't handle it. I wanted to. I just didn't want to be a distraction."

She made a frustrated noise. "Adrian, we've been in a relationship for three years!" She pointed a finger at my chest. "You're not a distraction. We're a team, and you lied to me." That hurt.

"I know." I caught my breath. "I thought I was doing the right thing. It's clear that I wasn't. I'm sorry." I looked at her. She was in disbelief.

"And business? I thought you had no interest in that. What's with the change of heart?" she asked.

"I tried telling Dad on the last day of school about changing plans, then he told me about his past, and a scholarship he lost. I didn't have the heart to tell him. Next thing I know, I got the call from CBU. He was so excited, and I chickened out, then avoided him. But I'm gonna tell him the truth. I want to travel with the band, with you."

I looked over at Mel as she took a long drag of her smoke, then finally exhaled.

"You know, a scholarship is a big chunk off of your shoulders," Mel reminded me.

"Is it, though? I mean, that's the same program Shay's in. Besides, I don't even know if I wanna do this."

"This isn't an opportunity that comes every day."

"You sound exactly like Mr. Price."

"No. I'm sounding reasonable," Mel cut me off. "I know what I said at prom. Then I heard what happened

63

at the show. University is huge, and having a scholarship puts you ahead of everyone else. This isn't an opportunity you can just throw away. I know the world isn't easy for you. Especially here."

All those things were true. The older I got, the more visible those interactions became. I didn't always like going to the shows Mel wanted to go to when we first started dating. I was always the standout. The one people thought would be a problem. It wasn't until I started drowning it out, and owning my space, that I started to enjoy it. Even then, things like the poster incident weren't new. Sure, it might have been the most overt thing to have happened, but it wasn't surprising, just terrifying.

"I worry about you. Even when you don't want me to." She began to fix my tie.

"I just didn't want to let you down with the tour," I told her.

"It's not all about me." It sounded like it hurt for her to say. Mel had been trying to convince me for months to come along.

"What about . . . us?" I asked.

Mel didn't answer. Instead, she lit another cigarette.

"After my parents split, Dad had custody of me," she finally said. "Things were pretty good for a while. I knew my parents weren't happy together. They always fought, over money, over everything. When they lived in different places, I got to see the best of both of them. Mom used to cook meals every Friday night, and play on her piano or guitar. We had a lot of fun that lasted us through the weekend. That's what I remember most. And I got to learn about my family overseas," she said. "I told you my grandparents were from India but I never told you where. They're from a place called Chennai, in the east. I only met them once while they visited when I was young. After they left, all I had were Mom's stories, and the photos she had when she went as a kid. She had always told me she would take me there one day. Me, being overdramatic, always adored the idea of going on a journey with someone I loved."

Mel took another drag of her smoke. "Fast forward," she said, exhaling. "One day, Dad dropped me off after karate. I walked up to the front steps, and Adrian . . ." I could see tears in her eyes. "She was gone. Just no sign of her."

Mel looked really hurt. She'd never told me that before. I knew it was a touchy topic, and I always assumed she'd tell me when she was ready.

"We heard from her a couple weeks later. She was in Toronto. I was alone. Not just without a mom. I felt like I was lost, without an identity. I don't have any family on my mom's side here."

Wow. Mel didn't have anyone to remind her of . . . herself.

Growing up mixed was by no means easy. I knew Mel faced some identity issues, like me, but also not so like me. Both my parents are half Black and half white, so I guess I never really felt like I was missing a side.

"So, in a way, I discovered punk to create my own identity. That's what it's about, right?" Mel shrugged. "I went to a show and met Kara. She was in a band called

Harbor Girls. Little did I know she basically got kicked out the night of a show."

"Why?" I'd heard of Harbor Girls before. I remembered meeting a girl named Steph from the band one time.

"They thought she was getting too political. She was writing about the issues Black and Indigenous people face. The issues she faces. She's a badass Black and Mi'kmaw guitarist, and never wants to shy away from it. But the band didn't wanna be known for that," Mel told me. "Harbor Girls is a band of suburban white girls who made a name for themselves being 'woke' until it came to race."

Both of Kara's identities meant a lot to her. Knowing they used her as a token was gross.

"After that we found Jade," Mel went on. "Jade moved from North Preston when she was well into her emo phase. Thank god we converted her to punk. Jade is the shy, quiet one. She's the best bass player I've ever met.

"Then Azra came along. People see the glasses, and the hijab and try to make assumptions. But every time she rocks out on those drums, she shows everyone that you don't have to be a certain way to be yourself. The four of us, a band of misfits and women of colour, made this promise not to apologize for who we are. Instead we make the world accept our identities, regardless," Mel said confidently. "Now Mom comes back, out of the blue, trying to break the progress and unity me and these girls created."

"Why did she leave?"

"I guess she wasn't ready. She was never ready to be a wife or a mother. Or anything." Mel looked off into the distance. "I guess if I never got the chance to go on our trip, maybe I can still go on a journey with others I love. Just someplace different."

"You didn't deser —"

"I know I didn't deserve it. It took me awhile to learn that." Mel looked at me, wiping her eyes. "When I met you, it taught me what a healthy relationship looks like, and I'm so happy you have this opportunity, Adrian." Mel gave me a big hug. I gave her a big squeeze back because it's what she needed.

"What I'm trying to say is, don't just jump on my ship because it's tempting to sail this direction." She let go. "You have options."

"So, you think I should just give up and join business admin?"

"No," Mel said. "I'm saying you ride this out until a bigger opportunity comes. You'll get into community studies, and when you do, make that jump with the scholarship money. Do what you want to do. Not what your dad wants you to. Make a promise to yourself, for your commitments, for the kids who were just like you, even if you have to endure a little discomfort along the way. It's worth it, you're worth it, and you can't let anyone tell you different."

That wasn't a bad plan. Whenever I get accepted into community studies, I'm sure I could make the change without a hitch. Maybe I wouldn't even have to tell Dad right away. I could see where Mel was coming from.

"I'm just a little relieved this time," she said.

"Relieved? Why?" I asked.

"Because at least I know when we might change paths."
She stepped on her smoke. "At least we can enjoy this summer, in between high school and university and tours. At least we can have this one thing. The summer between us."

CHAPTER 6

Boxes

I was pretty nervous about starting my first day at work, but Bobby put me at ease when I got to the library that morning. We had been contacting each other through email for the past couple months to discuss how we were going to approach a set of sessions called Unpacking Masculinity at the North Branch Library. It was our second summer doing it. Last year went without any major issues, and this year he wanted me to take more of a leadership role. I was eager to hopefully talk about eating disorders with the young guys, maybe use some of the things I learned from my ED group. Bobby told me we could definitely have that be one of our later sessions in the program. He even asked if I'd make a presentation. But for the very first session of the summer, Bobby wanted to jump right into the conversation about race.

"We all grow up with an unconscious bias," Bobby told the guys' group, "which leads to some folks being treated different than others."

Bobby was a white dude with a short buzz cut and always wore a Raptors jersey. Maybe he was a little too eager to talk about racism, but I appreciated how upfront he wanted to be with the guys. The group was mostly junior high students from across the city and each week we had a different topic to dissect.

He was explaining what unconscious bias meant while I looked around the room, kind of wishing I had a place like this when I was growing up. However, part of the work we did was to make sure we created the spaces we didn't have.

"I'm sure Adrian can speak to some of this." Bobby looked over at me. The entire group had our chairs formed in a circle. "He was telling me earlier today he had an incident this past weekend."

"Oh, uh, yeah," I caught myself as all eyes moved in my direction. "I was at my girlfriend's concert this past weekend, and these security guards accused me and my friend of stealing some posters." It was always better to be honest with young people about the lived experiences a lot of Black folks face. I'm sure some of them in this group, even at the ages of thirteen, fourteen or fifteen, could relate.

"Why'd they accuse you of stealing?" a kid named Dylan asked sarcastically. "You ain't about that life."

The group of guys laughed, and I did too.

"You might know that, though a lot of people assume otherwise. What we're getting at is that I was profiled,

70

simply for having the same skin colour as whoever did steal the posters."

"Those bouncers were assholes," Dylan replied.

"Language," Bobby cut in.

"Clowns. Those guards are clowns," Dylan corrected.

Dylan was right about that. The bruise on my arm had faded, and I thought I was over it. But honestly, I woke up that morning just feeling angry about it. Who were they to put their hands on Donny and me? I was sure I'd be angry about it for a while.

"My brother was stopped by cops two nights ago," Lenny spoke up.

"Why?" another teenager named Isaac turned to ask.

"He was just walking home; it was the second time it happened this month."

"Was he wearing a hoodie?" Isaac asked. "Maybe he seemed suspicious?"

"Hey, it doesn't always matter if someone is wearing a hoodie or seems 'suspicious,'" I said. "All that matters is that he was minding his business, and he got stopped."

Isaac's face instantly turned red. I didn't want him to feel embarrassed. I just wanted to be real, and that was the reality of Halifax. Halifax sometimes felt like a place not meant for a person like me, but that didn't mean I wanted to leave. It was my home, and I wanted to stick around and try to make it better. I just wish Dad could see that. He was so eager for me to get out of here. Before I could continue, my phone began ringing. I checked it quick, and it read Cape Breton University Admissions.

"Sorry, Bobby. I'll be one second," I said.

"Take your time, Adrian." Bobby smiled.

I was going to call them after the session. I guess they were even more eager than I was. Mel's plan made sense, and I'd stick to it. It didn't exactly ease my doubt. I hid behind a bookshelf, trying to be quiet, but still felt shaky when the admissions employee told me, "Yes, Mr. Carter. We need a confirmation no later than today or we have to move on."

If I said anything besides yes, I knew I'd let Dad down. I had to come to terms with this not being about him. It was my future, after all, and I was sure there'd come a time when I could switch over to community studies. That didn't mean I wasn't full of doubt. I just had to make a move. I turned to the community poster wall, and saw the sign for Unpacking Masculinity: Monday, Wednesday and Friday mornings. I was excited to pursue this work with Bobby for the time being, and if I could keep doing this in the future, then I had to take a chance. So I said, "Count me in."

Okay, I shouldn't have been as dramatic.

"Err . . . Okay," the woman replied. "I'll send you an email along with tuition details, dorm room information and facility tour dates. Have a great day, Mr. Carter. We look forward to seeing you this September."

"Thank you, have a great day," I said, hanging up the phone.

Bobby and I continued the session, and I was really happy with how it went. We got to hear from other teens who'd faced similar experiences. It was relatable, and somewhat validating. It didn't make it great though. A lot of us had similar moments like when we'd walk into a store and feel the need to buy something in case a cashier thought we were stealing, cops slowing down when they drove near us, or people making assumptions before they even knew us.

A lot of these kids never got the chance to talk about that in other spaces, so I was happy to help make a place where they could. As we neared the end, Bobby went over how the summer would play out.

"Topic four, we're having a session on mental health. We're gonna bring in a specialist for that. Topic five, we're going to chat about . . ." Bobby paused. "Effects of marijuana."

The guys laughed at him. "Yeah, yeah, yeah. We gotta take this one seriously, guys. Too many of y'all are too young for all that." Bobby was trying to be cool. "And to end the summer, Adrian is gonna helm a session on eating disorders among men."

"Men don't get eating disorders," Lenny laughed as I frowned.

"Hey, you never know. Adrian might add some perspective. He joined kickboxing and lost a ton of weight."

I didn't appreciate the "ton of" comment.

"Yeah, but it sounds like Adrian lost weight like a guy should. Not by sticking fingers down his throat!" Isaac laughed along with the others. I darted my eyes at him, and his face turned into a frown.

"Can we do a session on career training instead? I was hoping you could help me rework my resume," Dylan suggested.

I froze. None of these guys wanted to hear anything about eating disorders. That was the work I wanted to specialize in, and there was a group of kids just . . . laughing at me. I wish I could say it didn't hurt, but it did. Maybe this place wasn't as comfortable as I thought. Bobby told me earlier how excited they were for me to come back for the summer. I was curious if they would think of me differently if they knew what I'd been through or about the other work I did online.

"Hey, guys, let's take this seriously," Bobby cut the chatter when he noticed my face. "You never know who's in the room. Remember that, okay?" He looked around. "With that, I'll see everyone on Friday."

Afterward, Bobby assured me the kids in the group would come around. But I kept worrying about if they didn't. What if they continued to make fun of and undermine the struggle? I couldn't tell them I faced that. Not yet, at least. It was revealing that they were more open to hear about my experience with racism but I was more than that.

* * *

While leaving, I walked past the Unpacking Masculinity poster. Beneath it, I noticed something that wasn't there before. It was a Brown, Black & Infamous poster with the word HYPOCRITES written across it. That was one of the stolen posters from the show.

I ripped it down immediately. Whoever put it up couldn't have been far. I started looking around the library, sneaking near shelves and keeping an eye on the entrance. Eventually I made my way toward the printers and saw the culprit.

"Shay!" I called his name as he was printing off a document. I looked in the printer to see it was a CBU residence form, and beside that was his bag with the posters stuffed inside. "You stole these from the show?" I took his bag.

"Mind your own business." He tried grabbing his bag back, but I didn't let him. I pulled it away, causing the rest of the posters to fall out.

"You're the one putting these up?" I looked directly at him. "Me and Donny got blamed over this."

"Oh yeah? I'm sure it'll give you some clout, huh? You brag to those kids about being a victim?"

"Screw you," I growled. "Some great representation you are. How are you the valedictorian, senior student vice president, then steal posters from a band who are trying to make it by?"

"Ha!" Shay laughed. "You're the biggest hypocrite I know, Adrian. Unpacking Masculinity? Really? Did you tell them how you and your friends ruined my ride?" I bit my tongue. He had a point. "Then you have the nerve to accept this scholarship with no direction," Shay continued. "I know so many other people who would use that and make something of themselves."

"Who says I won't?"

"I do. You can't even stand on your own two feet without that shit band. Keep those posters if you want. I already have them scanned." He kicked them, then took his application. "You didn't even speak up in class to say you received the same scholarship meant for people who look like us, but never second guess hitting up punk shows filled with people who don't. And your friend says I'm the one trying to impress white kids."

Ouch. Shay was mixed, like me, and those comments were never good to hear.

"What shows I go to are none of your business," I said.

"You're right. I don't give a shit what you do. I give a shit about who gets what scholarship, because that's a responsibility, and you're clearly not up for the challenge." He pointed my way. "I have no idea why anyone thought you would be. If you can't handle this type of opportunity, stop pretending that you can," he said, grabbing his bag. "You can't be a role model if you're doing shitty things. That makes you a hypocrite at best. The difference is, I'm not pretending to be something I ain't." Shay left.

I picked up the posters and shoved them into my bag. I tried not to let what he said get to me, but who was I kidding? It did.

★ ★ ★

I let thoughts of my confrontation with Shay carry me into the evening. Mel had invited me for dinner with her mom. Martin was staying late at the music shop, and Prisha wanted to get to know me a little better. Honestly, I felt so awful about the dinner with our folks that I was hoping I could make up for it.

"Earth to Adrian?" Mel waved her hand in front of my face.

"Hey." I brought myself back in front of a plate of nachos.

"Melody tells me you had your first day at work. How'd it go?" Prisha asked.

"It was great!" I gulped down some water. "Everything went . . . great." I sighed.

I could see Mel's eyes linger. She knew I wasn't being truthful.

"Well, that sounds extremely interesting, Adrian. You're quite the storyteller," Mel said sarcastically. I smirked.

"Oh, yeah? How was your day?"

"My day was great!" Mel announced. "We had band practice, wrote a new song while waiting to pick you up, and now I'm stoked we have nachos." She motioned to her plate. "I'm just glad you didn't make them."

I blushed immediately.

"Oh, is there a story here?" Prisha asked with a grin.

"Please don't," I begged.

"Matter of fact, there is." Mel ignored me. "The first time Adrian made me nachos, he flooded the pan with cheese and apparently didn't have time to grab green peppers, chicken or even avocados. He used hotdog wieners."

Prisha almost spit out her water and laughed. Mel had a devilish smile. Okay, it wasn't my proudest moment.

"Did they announce the location for finals night yet?" I asked, changing topics.

"Some warehouse in Burnside."

Prisha raised an eyebrow in distaste. "Is that safe?" she asked.

"Depends who you ask." Mel shrugged.

She wasn't kidding. Before Mel dropped Shay in heels

on prom night, there was this guy who bullied me in grade ten. Mel knocked him out cold. He was so embarrassed he had to switch schools.

"I'm just saying, I don't think I like my daughter going to places like that."

Mel raised an eyebrow, and honestly so did I. It was pretty bold of Prisha to say things like that after being absent during Mel's teenage years.

"Maybe after the competition you can switch gears and try to get into Dal for a winter term?"

"We're gonna win this, then I'm going on tour," Mel said definitively.

"I think we need to have an honest conversation. That's why I wanted Adrian to come over tonight."

Oh boy. I took a breath.

Mel's eyes widened as Prisha went on. "Look at how well he's doing for himself. He's focused on studies, he's working part time and he's —"

"Constantly feeling stuck in awkward situations." I looked down at the floor. If only Prisha knew how much stress I was struggling with, she might change her tune. I'm guessing she must have spoken to my parents while I chased after Mel, and somehow, still, Dad is creating a chain reaction of awkward situations I have to navigate.

"Adrian, can you wait for me outside?" Mel said in a tone I hadn't heard before.

★ ★ ★

I could hear them going back and forth while I sat on the porch. It was pretty bad, and I felt really weird being stuck in the middle of it.

"Mel, can we just be reasonable for a minute?" I heard Prisha through the window.

"Reasonable?" Mel shouted. "You disappeared for YEARS! No! I can't be reasonable."

Parents were rough, no matter which way you cut it. I couldn't believe Prisha wanted me to come over to convince Mel out of the competition. That stress was the last thing she needed.

"If you're coming with me, get in the car." Mel slammed the door behind her as she got in the Camaro. I jumped in the passenger seat as she hit the gas.

"How dare she? She left me when I was a kid. Now she's come back acting like everything is going to be A-okay, like she can tell me what I want to do with my life. Who does she think she is? Do you know how heartbroken I was? How much I wanted a mom?"

Mel drove down to Point Pleasant Park and parked right in front of the harbour.

"Why is life so hard?" she asked, leaning her face on the steering wheel.

"I'm s —"

"Stop." Mel pressed her forehead against the horn and it echoed through the empty parking lot.

"What?" I was startled by the horn.

"Apologizing for things you can't control." She lifted her head, trying to calm herself.

We sat for a few minutes, just admiring the water. We

weren't too bothered by silence, as long as the view was pretty good. Mel went to grab a smoke, and I gave her a look, which caused her to sigh and throw the cigarette out of the window.

"I'm trying, okay?" She sounded stressed and took a deep breath. "I want you to be honest this time around. How was your day?" she asked, avoiding the conflict with her mom.

"Wild." I took a breath. "I found your missing posters."

"Whoa, what?" Mel sat up. "Who took them?"

"Shay." I sighed. "They're at my place."

"That little — ugh!" Mel hit the dashboard.

"Then he told me I didn't deserve the scholarship."

"Yeah, because Shay Smith is the only person in the universe."

"And before that, the kids in the group thought my session on eating disorders was dumb," I confessed.

"What?" Mel was shocked. "They should be stoked that you want to work with them. Look how far you came."

"Yeah, but they don't know that." I shrugged. "I froze, and it just makes me feel like I'm not ready to do this, no matter how much I do online."

"Online or in person, the work still matters, and you're the one doing it." She grabbed my hand. "And Shay is no moral compass, don't let these rich kids gaslight you into thinking what you should be. You know who you are. Someone to be proud of."

If only I could see myself the way Mel saw me.

CHAPTER 7
A Reality to Unpack

My plan was to make sure the guys' group became open-minded about my session on eating disorders. Maybe I had to work on being wittier like Bobby, or sterner to make a point. I would definitely try to practice my approach in front of the mirror.

In the meantime, I was logged into the recovery group, talking to some of the teens. Unlike at the library, I really felt like I had nothing to hide when speaking about my experiences and struggles here. This time around, the kids finally felt comfortable enough to open up about their experiences.

My name is Michelle. I'm fourteen years old and step on the scale more times a day than I have meals. I feel totally controlled by it, and I don't know what to do.

Name's Jay. I'm fifteen, and I'm always stress eating. My mom and dad just went through a divorce a few months back, and I haven't had any time to really process what happened. Kids at school are always saying shit to me, calling me a pig and a fatass. It's only making it worse.

I'm Tina. I just turned thirteen years old, and I don't eat during the day. When it's late, I eat almost everything I can find. Afterward, I well . . . I purge. I can feel changes. I'm getting smaller, my hair is getting thinner, and I have barely enough energy to make it through the day.

It was one of the most intense sessions I had with that group, and it made me so angry knowing how quick those kids at the library threw this topic under the bus. Bobby was right when he said you never know who's in the room. I spent most of the evening giving these teenagers the best advice I could. By the time it was over, I put my head down on my desk. It was worth it, even if it was emotionally draining. I heard a notification from the group app and looked up to see a message from Jay.

Hi Adrian, thanks for the peer support tonight. I know I'm the only guy in this group, and I was worried that'd be a problem before joining. You made me feel like I can open up about this, and I don't have too many spaces where I can say that. So I wanted to say thank you. This isn't easy, but I'm going to stick through.

See you next week,

Jay

It was moments like that which made it worth it.

"Hey, A?" Dad opened my door, and I shut my laptop immediately.

"What's up, Dad?" I spun my chair around. *He really needs to start knocking.*

"Not too much. Your mom is over at your grandmother's," he said awkwardly.

"Cool," I replied, followed by a silence.

Silence was an invisible wall between us, and we both weren't great at tearing it down.

"Hey, listen. The fights are on. I just put some popcorn in the microwave. I was wondering if you wanted to come watch? I know I'm not as fun as a punk show, or whatever it is you go to. But some time with your dad never hurt?"

I grinned. "Sure. Tell me who's on the card."

Dad and I sat in the living room watching two guys fighting in an octagon. Sounds barbaric, however I was always somewhat of a fan.

"You ever think of getting back into kickboxing?" Dad asked.

I used to train at a kickboxing gym called King's when I was sixteen. Mom was never a fan of me joining. I learned a lot about myself and a lot about discipline. It was a big part of my weight loss. Mel and I both went there for most of grade ten. We drifted away from it before the summer hit. I met a lot of great adults who motivated me to get into shape, but I wasn't getting results fast enough, and because of that, I, well, became bulimic.

"I miss King's, but I kinda feel like that's over with," I told him honestly. By the time Mel and I got to grade twelve, we were both more concerned with making memories than training. Besides, it was cutting into the other work I was ready to pursue.

"You never know." Dad sat up. "You could Google and see if there are any kickboxing gyms up in Cape Breton. You know what they say with university and the freshman fifteen." Dad patted my back, and I tensed up.

"Dad . . ." He caught wind of my tone, and his face turned red.

"I get it, still a sensitive spot. Pretend I didn't say that." He shook his head.

I hated those subtle comments. They dug deep, regardless of if it was intended or not.

Dad got up and went to the kitchen. He came back with two beers, popped them both open and put them in front of us.

"You wanna have a cold one with your dad?"

I laughed out loud, causing a frown to form across his face.

"What's so funny?"

"You know Mom would kill you."

"Yeah, well, your mother will never find out," he replied. "C'mon, have a beer with your dad. We won't get too many more moments like this."

Yeah, university is gonna change things.

I took the beer and sipped on it.

"This is disgusting."

"Never said it tasted great." Dad shrugged while taking a drink. "I'm not going to pretend this isn't what you and Donny will get up to at CBU, and I'll be damned if my son sneaks beer into college dorms before having one with me." We clinked our bottles together.

Dad was always around, mostly distant. He was always up early, gone to work before I went to school, sometimes not even home until after I went to bed. I was never upset about it, but knew he felt bad. Dad never got a university degree, and mortgages didn't pay themselves. He wanted to change that during my senior year; he made it a point to show up more. That didn't mean it was any less . . . awkward.

"So, your mother tells me you help some guy named Billy run a group for young men."

"Bobby," I corrected. "Yeah, it's at the library."

"What's it called? Talking . . . manhood?"

"Unpacking . . . masculinity." I sighed with embarrassment. I kind of wished Dad never knew about this group. He definitely wouldn't be the first person in line to sign up for it. Even if he should.

"I see," Dad said. "Something like that is a lot softer than . . . kickboxing."

"Yeah, and?"

"I just never seen the need for things like that. All we hear these days is toxic masculinity this and that. The last thing we need is our boys getting soft. If they get soft, they get lazy. If they get lazy, they get weak. That's not how things get done."

"I'm not weak," I told Dad, feeling frustrated. It was like he always had one foot in his mouth. He always had to find a way to imply I was soft. I could still enjoy watching a few fights or hitting some pads without a macho man mentality.

"I know . . . It's just . . ." Dad sighed. "I worry about you, y'know?"

"Why?" I didn't mean to ask so quickly.

"I, uh . . . I know what happened after you left kick-boxing. These days you have your friends, the shows you go to. I'm afraid you might fall back into where you were before."

"Where I was before?" Was he afraid of me gaining weight? Turning the freshman fifteen into the freshman fifty?

"Adrian . . ." Dad looked at me seriously as he took a breath. "The walls in this house are thin."

"The walls in this house are . . ." I repeated in confusion, then it hit. He wasn't so worried about me gaining weight.

"I know what you were doing, A. To lose . . ." He nodded to my stomach. I was too stunned to speak. He'd never mentioned it before, he never tried to help, he just . . . let it happen.

"A, I know you weren't expecting that. I know it was rough, and I was going to talk to you. I was just waiting for the right time. Then one day I came home, the scale in the bathroom was gone, and I stopped hearing you . . ."

He stopped hearing me purge at night. I felt my stomach turn.

"Then a short time after, you seemed happier, healthier. Your hair wasn't as thin as it was. And you finally looked comfortable in your skin. I was always so focused on work, staying late, going early, that I wasn't there when I needed to be," he said. "I'm worried you might fall back into old habits up there."

86

"Old habits? Really?" I was beyond pissed. "You think this is fine to tell me after I struggled with my body for years and pretend that it's suddenly okay?"

"I just . . . I just don't want you to have any distractions."

"What I was dealing with wasn't a distraction!" I yelled at him. "Me being bulimic had my full attention. You never thought to try to get me some help? Counselling? Anything?"

He didn't respond. He just sat there, embarrassed.

"Enjoy the fights." I went upstairs to grab my bag. The posters were still in there but whatever. I tried to make my way to the door, but Dad was waiting at the bottom of the steps.

"A, don't be like this. I didn't mean for it to come off like that."

"Well, it did!" I yelled, furiously grabbing my coat. "I gotta go."

Just a distraction? Even though I didn't purge anymore, how I felt about myself didn't change. It's not like I have six-pack abs, or a beach body. I have excess skin and I hate looking at myself in the mirror, or even taking off my shirt. I try not to hate parts of myself anymore, but that was the one thing I couldn't find it within myself to love. I've spoken to doctors, some of them hopeful, some of them not. I was told surgery would cost more than I can imagine, and one even said it should go back to normal on its own. It's been two years and I'm still in the same spot I was. Knowing he knew about it made my skin crawl. The most vulnerable parts of myself were a thin wall away, and he didn't even try to help. I don't know if I would have wanted him to. A gesture is better than nothing.

I texted Mel because I had to talk to somebody. Anybody.

> **Me:** You awake?
> **Mel:** Yeah, what's up?
> **Me:** Dad being an out of touch, insensitive, ass.
> **Mel:** Come over, the back door's unlocked.

I rushed over, not even bothering going to the front. Mel's bedroom was through the basement. I made my way in.

"AC." Mel got up from her bed. "What's going on?"

"He knew," was all I could say. "He fucking knew."

"Who knew? What's happening?"

"Dad said he knew about me purging." I sat on her bed. "He knew, and he never did anything."

I felt so betrayed and hated how he patted himself on the back for finally just being present.

I didn't need him. I had Mel. I had Donny. I had Kara. I had Azra. I had Jade. It took me a minute to realize that only one of them would be with me after the summer. That made me feel even worse. I resented how excited Dad was about me getting the scholarship, getting into university. He wasn't there for me when I needed him. Like those kids online, I felt controlled by the scale. Nobody understood what I was going through, only Dad knew, but he never did anything to help and that made it worse.

We lay back in her bed while I told her what happened.

"I guess we both have the eternal struggle of dealing with distant, overbearing parents."

"Why do people treat us as disposable, then suddenly put the entire weight of the world on our shoulders?" I asked.

"One second we're surrounded by ghosts and distance, then all of a sudden our shoulders become mountaintops."

"That's the song that seems to be on repeat lately." Mel sat up. "I think the cure to that is sometimes you gotta take the world and make it your own."

"How?"

"For starters, you have to learn to accept who you are." She intertwined her fingers with mine. "Know that your past is never anything to feel ashamed about. You made it so far, and there's so much further to go," she said. "Your dad let you down, just as my mom did to me. But that doesn't take away from how resilient you've become. Maybe I'm not the best person to be saying this, but you should never feel like you have anything to hide. You should embrace it. So what if a couple of teenage boys were laughing at your session? Or finding out your dad is out of touch and sucks at communication? All that matters is, you're open enough to have other people going through the same thing be open to you. Like that guy, Jay. Making it so at least one person can be open creates a world of a difference, and sure, it may be thankless at times, but just know the work you do matters."

I wrapped my hand around hers. *The work I do matters.*

"Thanks, Mel, I really needed that," I said as she kissed my cheek.

"I know, I'm the best. Ain't no big deal," Mel said sarcastically as she turned the lights off. I big spooned and rested my eyes. It didn't take long for our sleep to be interrupted by Mel's phone ringing.

Mel picked it up. "Hello?"

"Mel!" I heard Kara's voice. "Did you see what Shay posted?"

"What?" I turned the lamp back on.

"Posted what?" Mel sat up.

"Check the event page for the next round," Kara sounded stressed.

I took out my phone and went straight to the event page. There was a post with their poster that had HYPO-CRITES written over it in big letters. Below it, Shay's post read:

Brown, Black & Infamous claim to be an inclusive, punk rock band that fights for equality in a punk scene, yet engage in destruction of property, gate-keeping identity and have disdain for anyone who isn't a follower.

Below Shay attached photos of his flooded SUV.

"That asshole! Ugh!" Mel yelled as she jumped out of bed. "You and the band coming over?"

"We're already on our way," Kara replied.

Great . . .

Mel made coffee for the band as they occupied the basement.

"Is he trying to ruin our rep before finals?" Azra placed her hands on her head.

"Sounds like it." Jade was anxiously drinking her coffee.

Kara took the coffee away from her. "Jade, I love you, but coffee is the last thing you need right now."

Jade nodded while pulling her hair.

"We gotta hit him back," Mel told the band. "We gotta hit him hard, fast and unexpectedly."

"How?" Azra shrugged. "Going back and forth in a social media battle isn't exactly a great look."

"You're right. It isn't a great look," I cut in. "For what it's worth, I took your posters from him at the library." I opened my bag and as I took out a stack of them, a small piece of paper fell out of the pile. It was a poster that wasn't the band's.

Kara swiped it, and her eyes widened.

"Whoa, looks like you had buried treasure in there." She waved it around.

"What?" Azra took it out of Kara's hand. "Yo! This is a poster for a house party."

Mel snatched it to read what was on it. "3AM featuring DJ Dreamer, hosted by Shay Smith." She grinned. "A couple weeks away, just enough time to plan a surprise appearance," Mel announced. "Shay's gonna find out that he messed with the wrong girl gang."

CHAPTER 8
No Invitation Required

It turned out to be a girl gang plus two. Mel said she needed me and Donny for this plan to work. I was really hesitant about being involved. Honestly, I was nervous. Donny, on the other hand, loved the idea. I knew I couldn't stop my friends, so I guess I had to be damage control.

I rode with Mel and Donny. Azra, Kara and Jade were gonna meet us in the van. We made our way just outside the city, near a park called The Dingle, past the West End. Large homes lined up against a wooded area that eventually brought us close to a house next to a lake. It was Shay's. Mel parked down a path near some trees, not too far away.

"This guy lives out here?" Donny asked, surprised as he got out of the car.

"Looks that way." I was surprised to see how fancy the neighbourhood was.

"It's clear he doesn't need a scholarship." Donny was in awe.

"Nor does he need to punch down," Mel said, walking toward Kara's van. She knocked on the back door and Azra popped her head out with a grin.

"What are y'all doing in there?" Mel asked.

"Dressing for the occasion." Azra threw a blazer to Mel.

Kara hopped out the front with Jade. "Looks like we're stealing 3AM's spotlight tonight. We need to dress the part."

"Cosplaying as generic bro one, two, three and four?" Donny laughed.

"Seems poetic," I said nervously. "What happens when they show up?"

"They already did," Jade replied. "They did sound check earlier. I snuck around and noticed they left their gear so they didn't have to haul it around. According to their Instagram, they're doing a radio interview for College Campus Radio's night show. They're supposed to be back by midnight."

"And in the meantime, some DJ Dreamer is filler," Azra said.

I never heard of DJ Dreamer before, but I didn't envy him playing for the type of crowd that 3AM brings along: pretentious, privileged, assholes.

★ ★ ★

We made our way toward Shay's place. Cars were parked all along the road going to his parent's summer home. It looked like there were enough people there that we didn't

93

have to worry about not being invited. We'd blend in. There was no way we could go through the front door. Behind Shay's house was a lake where most of the party would be happening, so that was our entrance.

"There's his ride!" Jade pointed toward the gate.

"Time for phase one, the diversion." Mel brought us together.

We all approached the SUV and Donny dropped his bag from his shoulder. He had a handful of broken window stickers he passed to us. We started applying them. We weren't going to destroy any more of his property, but that didn't mean we weren't going to trick him.

As Donny and the gang chatted and applied the stickers, I couldn't stop thinking about Dad. We hadn't really spoken to each other since our argument. Communication was nothing more than a head nod or eye roll in passing. Mom knew something was up, but didn't say anything. I still couldn't get over what he said and how he went about it. It was so short-sighted and insensitive. Talking wasn't one of Dad's strong suits. Who am I kidding? It wasn't exactly mine either.

So I spent more time with the crew. It was difficult coming to terms with this maybe being our last summer together for a long time. I would rather be doing something more meaningful than focusing on Shay. I understood what Shay did was wrong, but I just felt like the more we'd go after him, the harder he'd come after us. None of these girls would have to see him every day at university.

"Hey, you okay?" Mel poked my arm and whispered. "You've been quiet all night."

"I'm fine."

"C'mon, we both know that's not true." She frowned.

"I'd just, rather be doing something other than damage control."

I didn't mean to sound like a jerk.

"You're not damage control," Mel replied. "If you only wanted to undermine this, then you didn't have to come along."

Before I could reply, Donny cut in.

"Hey, lovebirds. We don't have a lot of time before someone notices this. Let's get moving."

★ ★ ★

The next part of the plan was to make sure 3AM didn't show up. We all made our way to the lake. Drunk kids playing beer pong, smashing cans on their heads and making out made it easier for us to blend in. As we got closer to the back deck, I noticed Shay hanging out by his laptop on a stage while spinning records at a turntable.

"Whoa, is Shay the DJ?" Mel asked with a giant smile on her face.

"DJ Dreamer in the house!" His voice echoed across the wooded area. The girls along with Donny couldn't stop laughing and I cringed more than anything else. This guy made it way too easy.

"Yo!" some bro called over the techno beats. "Where's 3AM at?"

"They'll be here. I'm just warming up for them!"

"Boo!" a drunk girl yelled.

"Brutal." I watched.

3AM wasn't there, and as expected, I could see their gear, instruments and banners on the side of the small stage.

"I hope the boys don't mind us borrowing their stuff." Mel looked around. "Donny, AC, you see the laptop he's using? Cut the music off, delete what he posted about us, then lock his account. Azra, we won't have time to set up the drums, if you could call their interview at CCR and . . ."

"Fangirl out?" Azra was disappointed. "I suppose."

"In the meantime, Jade, Kara and I will hold the stage." Mel smiled.

It didn't take long for a dude in the crowd to shout, "Someone smashed Shay's ride!"

Shay's motions on the turntable stopped. His eyes widened and shoulders dropped.

"The anxiety has set in," Donny narrated.

"You better be lying!" Shay rushed off the stage, running with other drunk kids to see what happened.

"All right, let's go!" Kara yelled as we all ran to our designated spots. Donny immediately opened up Shay's laptop while I kept a lookout. The girls began setting up the equipment, and the few people who stayed around were either too drunk or didn't care about what we were doing.

Azra pulled out her phone and put it on speaker while dialling the number for the station.

"Looks like we have our last caller of the night," I heard the host say. "You have anything you wanna say about 3AM?"

"OMG? Is Chet there?" Azra over-exaggerated her excitement.

"Chet's here." He spoke about himself in third person.

"I just wanted to say that your EP about your crazy ex was amazing! What was your artistic process when writing it?"

Mel looked like she wanted to vomit when Azra said that.

"Looks like Shay got in a little back and forth with his dad." Donny smirked from the computer.

"C'mon man, you're not supposed to be checking his messages, just delete what he posted."

"This is too good to ignore," Donny said. "Take a look."

I shouldn't have, but I did. I looked at the message from Shay's father, who I didn't realize was white.

Bruce Smith:

Shay, I hope you're keeping the house in shape while I'm in Toronto. I've been thinking about what you were saying, about staying in Nova Scotia. Son, this is a mistake. I could help set you up in the University of Ottawa, Toronto, hell, even Harvard if we tried hard enough. You have a gift, and you're wasting it. This black entrepreneur collective you want to start up is silly. You've got to stop focusing on that nonsense. This idea is nothing short of a handout. That's part of the reason I didn't want you to accept this phoenix scholarship. Say the word and let's move forward.

Don't do anything stupid while I'm away.

Talk soon,

Dad

"I told you Shay was fake. He's just a rich kid who suddenly wants to be woke because it's trendy," Donny said. "I have no love for these trust fund kids."

"Donny . . . I don't think we should be looking at this." I clenched my jaw. I didn't realize Shay's father was such an ass. Not that I felt bad for him, it just felt too personal.

"He'll be fine, trust me." Donny switched tabs, deleting the post from Facebook. Instead of locking Shay's account, he looked at the groups Shay was the admin of. "Shay manages the BIPOC Graduation Group. You never know when access to something like this could come in handy."

"Keep on task, Donny."

"I'm just having some fun." He laughed while opening up some files on the computer.

"This isn't part of the plan."

"Shay's a musician now, right? I have a feeling there's gold here, and now we found some." He smiled as he clicked on a file named Vocal Practice for EP.

As soon as he opened it, our ears were met with what sounded like . . .

"Is that a dying animal?" Kara called over to us. It was really that bad.

"It's Shay's EP vocals!" Donny called back.

"Ohhh." Mel laughed deeply. "It'd be a real shame if that somehow got leaked."

"Come on, guys," I cut in. "Don't you think this is a little much?"

"Just like stealing our posters? Slandering us online? Blaming you and Donny at the show?" Kara shot back.

I looked over at Jade, who shrugged with agreement.

"Whose team are you on, Adrian?" Mel frowned at me again.

She didn't have to say that in front of everyone. It wasn't about teams. It was about right and wrong. I wasn't too concerned about Shay, but what he said kept twisting something inside my stomach. How could I be a role model if I was taking part in things like this? What would Jay say if he knew I was doing this? What would Bobby say? Shay went too far. But uploading something this personal didn't make it right.

"Whatever." I shook my head and kept watch. The band continued setting up 3AM's equipment, and Donny hit upload. "This may take a minute or two. So I suggest you start playing. Once this is done, everyone who follows Shay should get a notification."

"Sounds good to me," Mel said while plugging in the mic. "Test one, test one-two."

Some folks were heading back toward the lake, and Mel began strumming the guitar while Jade hit the bass and Kara came in too.

"We are Brown, Black & Infamous!" Mel yelled as more people came back. I shook my head and hopped off stage.

"Adrian, where are you going?" Donny called.

"I'm out," I called back and made my way out of there.

I passed everyone rushing to the lake as the three of them rocked out. Not long after, I received a notification about a new post from Shay — the audio file of his horrible singing.

"No! No! No!" I heard a voice cry out and quickly hid behind a bush. It was Shay, frantically pressing buttons on his phone. "My password was changed? How!"

Shay shook his head, threw his phone as far as he could and sat down, head in his lap. As much as I despised him for what he did, it was hard not to feel a little bad. Who wouldn't be an asshole with a dad like that?

Maybe I wasn't as bad off as I thought.

★ ★ ★

I walked for at least an hour as I made my way back toward the city. It was pitch-black, so I tried avoiding cars as best as I could. I heard a car slow down, and I turned to see a purple Camaro.

Mel rolled down her window. "There you are. You getting in or what?" She was alone. "C'mon, don't walk back to the city. You'll get attacked by a raccoon or two. I don't feel like waiting for you to get a rabies shot tonight."

That didn't sound pleasant, so I got in. Mel hit the gas and turned on the radio. They must've been replaying 3AM's interview on CCR, because we heard Chet's voice, "Hey, listen, lady, we appreciate you calling but we have a show to hit up."

"Oh, don't worry about that. A new band took your spot at Shay's house party."

"Wait, what?" Chet replied.

"We're called Brown, Black & Infamous. And just to be clear, I think all your music is trash. Learn to cry for once in your life or go to therapy, you misogynistic, broken, man-child!" A dial tone followed.

"Sorry about that," the host cut in. "As you can see, we are not invincible to trolls."

I laughed at that, and so did Mel.

"Look, I'm sorry I asked whose side you're on in front of everyone." Mel looked over at me.

"It's not about that," I sighed.

"I'm sure Shay is going to be A-okay."

"Yeah, and how far are we going to take this? You think he's not gonna try to hit us back?"

"You gotta stop being nice to people who wronged you. Why do you care so much?"

"Because I can't try to be a role model with Bobby and mentor online while doing things like this. I can't . . ." I took the words out of Shay's mouth. ". . . pretend to be something I'm not."

"Pretend to be something you're not? Okay," she responded quietly. "Got it. I'm sorry I got you involved."

The rest of the ride was full of silence, and not the comfortable kind. I couldn't stop thinking that maybe I was outgrowing my friends.

When Mel dropped me off, she mentioned, "Next week is your tour of the facility. You still want me to come?"

"Of course, if you want to make the trip." I got out.

"I guess I'll see you then." She pulled off without saying anything else. It took me a minute to realize that was a whole week away. That would be the first week of August, meaning the summer between us would be officially halfway over.

CHAPTER 9
Centre of the Universe

"Thanks for coming along," I said to Mel as I sat in her passenger seat. We had to be at CBU for noon, so we'd already been on the road for a few hours with my parents behind us. I had a lot on my mind. I still hadn't heard back about community studies, and we were getting way too close to the fall semester. On top of that, Mel and I hadn't spoken much since Shay's party. It made me worried. Sure, she was focused on practice and I was focused on the presentation for Bobby. But things just seemed off between us. I thought the space would help, but we just felt . . . distant.

"Hey, if it gets me away from my parents, I'm down. Besides, they weren't too upset to hear I'm going on a university tour." Mel faked a smile that was followed by silence. This still wasn't the comfortable kind we were used to. I looked over at her while her eyes were on the road. I wanted to say something, anything, but before I could, my voice got buried in Donny's loud yawn from the back seat.

"Well, if you do end up giving up music and coming out here, know that the homie already has a roommate." Donny patted my back. He decided to third-wheel us instead of bringing his parents all the way out.

"Yeah, I bet," Mel laughed. I could tell she rolled her eyes even if she wore sunglasses. We made a few pit stops and drank so much coffee I was shaking in my seat. I felt lucky we were getting close.

Once we drove past Sydney, things slowed down. We were eager to get out of the Camaro, and it didn't take long until we reached a Cape Breton University sign.

"Ehh, we're here!" Donny let out a sigh of relief.

Mel pulled into the parking lot with my parent's car close behind. I observed the outside of the University from the front seat, seeing how big it was. My view was interrupted by Donny kicking the back of my seat.

"Hurry up, my legs are jelly." He wanted to get out.

"Hold on." I got out while Mel grabbed a cigarette.

"This place is lit." Donny pulled himself from the car and patted my back. It was. It looked like a small town, if anything. Buildings lined the road, and I had no idea which one we were supposed to be in. The dorms at the end looked big. I only hoped the actual rooms would be big enough for me and Donny to survive together.

"Wow." Mom was in awe as she came up to me. "I guess maybe it was worth the drive. You feeling it yet, Adrian?"

"I guess so." I shrugged as Mel got out of the car and stepped on her lit cigarette.

We eventually found the right building, and inside seemed pretty crowded, even for August. I guess universities don't always slow down just because there are no students around. People sat in their offices on the phone, and at the photocopying machine. A young-looking white dude in a yellow shirt with a really big smile called us over to a group of other young people.

"You're the only one who brought their parents." Mel poked me, giggling, while I rolled my eyes.

"Good afternoon, future CBU students," our guide greeted us. "My name is Mike, and I'm happy to show you around the campus today. Each of you will be able to get your first glimpse of what our facilities have to offer."

The tour began in the main cafeteria. Definitely an upgrade from our high school. I hoped there would be fewer food fights too.

"Our cafeterias are open every day until six p.m.," Mike said. "Feel free to use this space to study and get to know your peers. After then, you can head over to the campus lounge. We have open mics, talent shows, lots of food too."

Next, we got to see the great hall. That's exactly what it was, a giant hall. I found it fascinating. On the ceiling, I saw flags from different countries students came from. It definitely helped diversify my thoughts on this place, because on the surface, Cape Breton seemed . . . pretty white. I was curious if there would be any African Nova Scotian student groups. If there weren't, maybe I could step up?

The tour then proceeded to the library. It was two floors and filled with books, computers and other resources. It felt very welcoming. A place where I could spend time studying. I had a feeling living with Donny would make this place a second home. One a whole lot less noisy.

Eventually we circled back outside and moved toward the campus lounge. I looked back to see Mel instantly side tracked by a path. She made her way toward a sign in front of it.

"Hey, sorry, miss, that place isn't ready yet!" Mike called.

"What's down that path?" Dad asked.

"They're building an observatory, which will hopefully be ready by late October or early November," Mike replied.

"Huh." Mel stared toward the path as I walked up. "Looks like you'll have a pretty good view."

You'd love this, I wanted to say, but was too afraid to. It made me worry that this was my future, a future without her. As beautiful as the campus was, I didn't think I could stomach going just because Dad or Mr. Price thought I should. The plan of waiting to switch programs was cutting way too close for comfort.

"Wow, man. This place has everything." Donny hung off my shoulder, patting my chest.

"Just one more month." Mom smiled. "We need to decide what you're taking and what you're leaving behind."

I hadn't even thought about that.

"Just remember it's a shared space," Donny laughed. "Let's go check out the dorms!" He began to walk away with my parents. I was going to, then I looked to see Mel's back turned to us, as she looked toward the path to the observatory. I started to follow her instead.

"You coming, Adrian?" I heard Dad ask. "If I'm chipping in for your dorm, can you at least pretend to be excited?"

"Just go." Mel looked over at me. "I'll catch up."

★ ★ ★

I convinced Donny to roll back with my parents because I had a feeling Mel wanted to talk.

"Nice school, huh?" She asked, eyes on the road. Mel looked distant, like there was more she wanted to say.

"Yeah . . . It looks like it has everything."

"Everything, eh?" she replied.

Bad choice of words.

"I mean . . . It doesn't have —"

"It has a late-night cafeteria, dorm rooms, a hella awesome observatory, a gigantic library —"

"It doesn't have you," I cut her off. She didn't reply. Instead, she focused on the road for a few moments, then took a turn off one of the exits that definitely didn't take us to Halifax.

"Yo . . . Where are we going?"

"Just trust me, okay?" She hit the pedal. "Relax."

"All right." I laid back in my seat.

By that point, I felt an adrenalin dump from all the caffeine. I was exhausted, not realizing how stressed I'd been as of late. My presentation on eating disorders was two days away, and sure, I had everything planned out, I just . . . didn't feel ready for it. But there, in Mel's car, I was finally able to shut my eyes. It didn't take long for me to fall asleep. I didn't know how much time had passed. I only remember waking up to her shaking my arm.

"Sleepy?" Mel smiled at me.

"Jeez, where are we?" I looked around to see the stars had already taken over the sky.

"We're close to my parents' cabin." Mel took the keys out of the car. "Thought maybe we could talk somewhere calm."

"Talk?" I asked.

"C'mon." She got out of the car.

I followed her down the path we were used to. We spent a lot of time at the cabin last summer, but we hadn't been there since. Mel liked to get away, and didn't always tell Martin we were hanging here. My parents didn't even know about this place, so I sent them a text telling them I was spending the night at Mel's so they wouldn't worry.

We found our way toward a river and climbed a tree that had fallen over. She grabbed my hand as we went across.

"Eyes on me." I knew she was smiling as I tried to keep my balance.

Once we made it across, we climbed the hill to see Martin's cabin below. "Why'd we come here?" I asked.

Mel let out a sigh. "I'm . . . just not ready to go back home, okay?"

"Oh." I felt bad for not cluing in. "How are things going with —"

"Can we not talk about that right now?" Mel sighed again.

"Okay, then what do you wanna do?"

"I wanna go for a swim." Mel took off her shoes and undressed. She was wearing a bathing suit underneath her clothes.

"You totally tricked me into coming here." I raised an eyebrow.

"Yeah, I guess I did." She shrugged as she walked toward the lake.

"Mel, the sun's down. It's probably cold," I tried to convince her, knowing she wanted me to jump in.

She grabbed my hand and started pulling me toward the water.

"Hold up!" I dragged my feet in the dirt.

The whole undressing thing always made me anxious. I had taken my pants off, but still wore my boxers. I looked over at Mel, then back to my black t-shirt. Being covered in excess skin made me look like I had a body I never grew into.

"I know," she whispered. "You can keep it on." She grabbed my hand as I followed her toward the lake.

She jumped in with no hesitation. Me? I stuck one toe in, which led to a foot, which led to a leg.

"Mel, it's kinda cold," I told her.

"Yeah, yeah, maybe you're right." Mel swam back toward me, extending me her hand. "Help me up?"

"Seriously?" I grinned.

"Hurry, help me get out of the water!"

I reached for her hand, then she grabbed my entire arm, pulling me into the lake along with her. I screamed when I fell in, and I looked up to see Mel sticking her tongue out while splashing me.

"Cut it out!" I laughed. "Mel, this is my only shirt."

"Luckily, you left your Citadel hoodie last time we came here."

"Wait, how'd you know? I was looking for that."

"Let's just say I plan ahead." She winked at me.

I laughed and swam toward her. She leaned in, giving me a hug. She held on to me while watching the water around us. The stars reflected off the water so light was never too far away.

"Okay." I looked around. "This is pretty great." I wrapped my arms around her. "What are you thinking about? I know there's something on your mind."

Mel didn't reply right away. She looked off in the distance, and I could see her lips curving into a smile.

"I'm thinking, this is the centre of the universe."

"Somewhere in Nova Scotia?" I laughed.

"No, dork. I mean wherever we meet."

I smiled when she said that.

"Listen, I'm sorry I've been distant lately," her voice was regretful. "I've just been thinking about what you said at Shay's party, about you pretending to be somebody you're not."

I really wish I'd used better phrasing when I said that.

"Mel . . . I'm sorry I said that."

"And I'm sorry I took it so far." She leaned against me. "I've been wrestling with that for a week. Especially with what you said about Shay's dad. Maybe he's not as different from us as we think."

"Maybe not."

"I guess even Shay Smith is capable of doing good

once in a while. You know what they say about broken clocks."

"Oh yeah? What about the second time?" I was curious.

"Let's not get too ahead of ourselves." She rolled her eyes. "Speaking of pretending to be someone you're not . ." Mel placed her hands on my shoulders. "I seen you at the university. You were hesitant about everything."

I'm glad she could read me better than my parents, but maybe it wasn't that hard to tell.

"You're supposed to start in a few weeks. This plan of just waiting for someone to drop out and getting into community studies isn't exactly looking likely right now."

"It isn't," I said honestly. "I don't really feel like jumping into a program my heart isn't in, just because I can."

In a perfect world, someone in community studies would have dropped out by now, and I'd be contacted to take their seat. That didn't seem to be the case anymore.

"Then don't go through with this," Mel told me.

"What about the scholarship?"

"Adrian?" Mel raised her eyebrow at me. "Screw the scholarship. You can't let it dictate your life."

"You said —"

"It's not about what I said. It's about what you want. Do you want to let those kids down?"

I didn't want to let Bobby or the teens down. The hardest part would be telling my dad I couldn't go through with it. He already mentioned he wanted to help contribute to my dorm with Donny, though I wasn't sure if I could bring myself to go. So, I guess in the meantime that meant . . .

"You should come with me, and the girls."

"What? Mel . . ."

"You gonna stay at home? With your overbearing, judgmental dad?"

"I . . ."

"Just think about it. We have the space, okay?"

"Okay." I finally let out a breath. "I'll think about it."

I should have asked Mel why she suddenly switched gears, but it wasn't exactly a moment I wanted to ruin. She pulled me into a hug, then swam back toward the cabin. I followed.

"Are we heading back to the city tonight?" I asked, shaking the water off me.

"I was thinking we could spend the night here. Away from the rest of the world. Just you and me," Mel said. "We spend so much time worrying about the future that we forget to make memories right here. Right now."

She pulled me toward the cabin, and once we dried off, she kissed my cheek and I saw a flash in front of my face.

"Pictures?" I laughed. "Really?"

That was followed by another flash.

"Yes," she said, taking the two photos from the camera. "Except this time. I want you to try something different. You take one photo, I take the other," she said as I grabbed the first.

"I thought you always gave it to the person you're taking a picture with."

"Maybe this is the memory I want to keep." Mel smiled at me.

As it developed, I could see my eyes looked surprised

while she buried a kiss in my cheek. I looked at hers to see I had a grin.

"Why do you get to keep that one?"

"Because that's how I wanna remember this summer."

CHAPTER 10
She Needs You

I woke up the next morning covered in blankets, arms wrapped around Mel. I felt her breath against my neck, and I didn't want to move. I was glad we got some alone time away from the stress and had a moment just for us. We got to hold onto the night a little tighter, instead of letting it slip through our fingers.

Mel woke up not long after, and buried herself in my chest, then moved up.

"Hey," I greeted.

"Good morning." She kissed me and wrapped her arms around me.

"Morning breath," I gasped.

"Deal with it." She went for another.

She squeezed me real tight then said, "I wish we could just stay here."

"Me too." I sat up. "I got the presentation with Bobby tomorrow."

"You're gonna kill it."

"I gotta finish the PowerPoint first." I stretched.

Mel let go and let out a long yawn. "Maybe we can come back in a couple weeks." She got up to get dressed, then said, "Don't get too comfortable. We do gotta hit the road eventually. I'm going for a smoke," she said as she left.

I laid back, not wanting to get up. I heard my phone lighting up with texts. It was probably Mom asking where I was. She knew I was in safe company.

I reached for my phone to see the battery was dead.

"Huh?"

I heard the notification sound go off again, and again and again. Then peeked over to the nightstand on Mel's side of the bed. Her phone's screen was lighting up. I probably shouldn't have checked, but I was more curious than I should have been. I moved over to see Martin and Prisha had been blasting her phone.

Dad: Mel, where are you? I told you to come home after.

Dad: You better not have gone to the cabin. I'll take those keys away.

Prisha: Melody, please call.

Prisha: Melody, your father and I want to have a serious talk later.

Dad: Melody.

Dad: You have some explaining to do.

Prisha: Just come home.

Shit. I put the phone down. A moment later, Mel came back in.

"Get dressed, lazybones." She threw my jeans at me from the floor. "Let's hit up a diner on the way back."

"Yeah, sure." I put them on. "Your phone was going off."

"I'm sure it's just Dad being Dad."

"Yeah, maybe." I put my sweater on. "Ready to head out?"

"Ready."

Mel wasn't exactly in a rush to get home. I was worried she might get in trouble, but I didn't want to pry. We took the long way and stopped by a diner just off the highway somewhere in Lower Sackville before she dropped me off. It was past four p.m. by the time we got back to the city.

When I got inside the house, I saw Dad making burgers. He looked up at me.

"There he is." Dad smiled. "So, what'd you think of the university? Pretty great, huh?"

Right. Awkward conversation ahead.

"Yeah, it looked great," I replied, taking a seat.

"Is that Adrian?" I heard Mom's voice as she came down the steps. "Listen, I know we still have a few weeks, but I already went ahead and began packing some things I know you'd forget."

I really wish Mom didn't do that.

"Forget? Like what?"

"I threw some shoes and fall sweaters in some boxes. It's a different kind of cold up there that I know you're not prepared for."

Dad began dishing out some burgers, while I had already lost my appetite. Things were still awkward between us. We never had the chance to hash things out. I'm sure he thought time would heal, but we had to address this instead of pretending it never happened. Right now had to be the time. I was full of anxiety, knowing I had to tell them the truth. I took a moment to close my eyes, and when I opened them, I finally spoke.

"Mom, Dad. I've been thinking a lot about this scholarship and starting at CBU. Honestly, right now isn't a good time. I'm wait-listed for a community studies program I want to major in, and if all goes well, I'd like to focus on working with young people, who are like me, who struggle with eating disorders." I looked over at Dad. "I know what you're going to say about wasting this scholarship. It's not the end of the world, I can promise you that." He dropped his burger and crossed his arms. "What I'm getting at is this, if I have to risk some loans, or work a little harder to build a community I want to take part in, it's worth it."

I looked over at Mom, who raised an eyebrow. "You know the work I've been doing with Bobby at the library, Unpacking Masculinity. When you suggested that last year, I couldn't have imagined it being as fulfilling as it is, but I learned things about myself I couldn't have found elsewhere. I feel like I'm meant for this type of work."

I took a breath. "I'm not off the waitlist, and it isn't looking like that's going to change. So maybe taking a year off isn't the worst idea in the world? I mean, in the meantime maybe I can live a little? Travel with Mel? Come back, get some more experience with Bobby? Work on a resume so by the time I'm done university I can be a shoo-in to work somewhere? I know this isn't what you expected, but I have to do this. For me."

That wasn't so hard, was it?

Of course it was hard. I never said any of it.

"Yeah, it probably does get really cold up there," I replied to Mom, coming to reality and forcing a smile. *Why am I so scared to let them down?*

"Hey, A?" Dad cut in. "Mind if I use your laptop a bit later? I have some fantasy football —"

"Sure, just give me an hour," I told him. The next day was going to be my last session of the summer with Bobby, and it was my turn to lead. I had a lot to catch up on.

After supper, I made my way to my room, finally plugged in my phone and decided to log in to my recovery group. There were some usual things going on. A teenager named Miranda was freaking out because she overate at a family get-together. Devon's hair had begun thinning because of her purging. I was doing my best to be present for them, knowing this was exactly where I was supposed to be.

On top of that, I was working on some slides for the session. I was pretty bad at PowerPoint, so I was trying my best to make my presentation entertaining. I was so nervous and couldn't stomach the idea of them bashing this again. Bobby gave me some pointers on how to own the room and the space we shared. Be confident, be assertive, be . . . *everything that isn't me.*

I laid my head on the desk to see my phone finally power up. As notifications began popping up, I realized I had missed an email from Cape Breton University Admissions.

I assumed it was just more dorm information until I saw the subject was community studies.

"Whoa." I instantly lifted my head and checked.

To Adrian Carter,

We have received a large volume of applicants for our Community Studies Program this past year. Your application has been selected from our waitlist in consideration of your academic achievement and contributions to your community. We are pleased to offer you placement in our fall semester. This email is time sensitive. Please contact us within a week's time to confirm your enrollment in the school of —

I picked up my phone and immediately dialled the admission office's number.

"Cape Breton University Admissions office, how may I help you?"

"Hi, this is Adrian Carter calling to follow up on an email."

"Adrian Carter . . . Let me look up some records." She typed away, searching for my file. My anxiety was through the roof. *Is this really happening?*

"Yes, we would like to offer you a seat in our community studies program, however it looks like you're registered in business administration."

"Is there a way to make a switch?" I knew I sounded eager.

"Yes, there is. You're currently with a scholarship, I see. It looks as though it was only put on an account instead of paid, so I can definitely transfer that over for you."

Oh my God. This is a dream come true. Thank you, universe. You sometimes get it right.

"Yes, please. Let's do that," I replied, not able to hold in my excitement.

"Sure thing, just be aware that we're closing up for the day, and it may take a day or so for a new confirmation email saying you're in the program. In the meantime, you will get an email saying you are no longer part of the School of Business."

"Thank you, thank you, thank you!" I had to cover my mouth.

I jumped back to my ED group, noticing the email notification that read Cape Breton University Admission Status.

I had to tell Mel. I switched tabs on my phone to send her a text.

Me: Hey, you around?

There was no response, and I was feeling jittery, nervous, full of anxiety and excitement. She must have been home. Maybe I could drop by really quick and tell her the news.

After my session, I snuck out while Mom and Dad were watching a movie on Netflix. I could tell them the news later, but I thought it important to touch base with Mel first. When I made my way to her front steps, I could hear Martin's voice echo all the way outside.

"You wasted all that time just to come back with nothing? Mel, life isn't just one big road trip. You can't just run away. You spent three years in the elite class, only to throw it away!"

"He's right, Melody," Prisha's voice filled the air. "This is ridiculous. Did you even pay attention during the tour?"

"I didn't go for the university tour, okay!" Mel snapped. "Maybe I just wanted to spend some time with my boyfriend before we inevitably break up, just like you said!"

My eyes widened, making everything else sink in like it hadn't before. Prisha really said that to Mel?

"Unlike both of you, he's not making me feel like shit over my decisions. He's not the one who puts me down."

"And who are you going to run back to once he's moved on?" Prisha shot back.

Not cool. I stood over by the window to see them.

"I'd be surprised if you'll be here, Mom. I didn't ask you to come back!" Mel yelled. "You can't just blame Dad for disappearing! So what if you weren't ready to settle down, or help Dad with his shop. You still had a daughter, you still had a responsibility and you ran away!" I could hear her voice crack as she let it all out.

There was a silence, and it didn't take long for Martin's voice to fill the air.

"Mel! That's enough. Regardless of what happened, you don't get to speak to your mother that way."

"You're the one who blocked her number after she ran away!" Mel pointed out. "You don't get to go back and forth on that, Dad."

"That's not the point, Melody." He sounded livid. "And you know what? If you want to waste your life, you won't do it on my dime. Your band won't be practicing in my shop, and you won't be using my cabin anymore either."

"Dad . . . You know finals night is coming up."

"That's not important to me. Your band is not important to me!"

I didn't need to see Mel's face to know what was on her mind. There was a silence that was deafening.

"Martin . . ." Prisha's voice finally cut in. "I don't think that was —"

"Prisha, stop it. She needs to hear it."

"Fuck you!" Mel yelled as the front door slammed open. I watched her march down the steps and get into the car, driving off. I was still in the bush, so she hadn't seen me.

When I finally stepped out, I heard Martin. "Adrian?" He came outside, putting on his glasses. "How long were you there?"

"Long enough to see how much of an asshole you are, Mr. Woods," I said. "You know how much this band means to her. Both of you."

"I thought someone as motivated as you could have put some sense into her." Martin crossed his arms, shaking his head.

"I think she has enough sense to do what she wants," I replied, getting in his face.

"Guys, stop." Prisha moved between us. "This isn't getting us anywhere."

"You know what else isn't getting us anywhere? Disrespecting her. Minimizing everything that's important to her." I turned to walk away. "How is this surprising to either of you!"

They both stood there, silent, Prisha's head down, Martin scratching his head.

"Maybe think on that while I go find her."

★ ★ ★

She wasn't on the rooftop or at Martin's store. I called Azra because I didn't know who else to turn to.

"Damn, she came to my place after she dropped you off. You must have got there when she was getting home. I can't believe Martin said that to her. Want me to drive down? We have to find her."

Mel must have been avoiding her parents for a reason. That was why she wanted to come to Cape Breton.

"I'm fine." I was walking down toward the waterfront. "I tried texting her, but I don't know where she'd go. Can you check Dreamer's Corner? Redemption House?"

"Got it," Azra reassured me. "Please tell me if you see her. If anything happens to her —"

"I know," I replied. "I will. Thank you, Azra."

"Anytime, Adrian. Stay safe."

I hung up and noticed the Tim Hortons was closed. That shut down any theories of her drowning her sorrows in an Iced Capp, but I saw a familiar vehicle on the other side of the restaurant. It was a Camaro. And it was purple.

"Mel!" I called as I ran toward it. She wasn't there. "Where are you?"

I heard a buzzing and turned toward the ferry terminal.

"Dartmouth ferry, now boarding," said an automated robotic voice.

I ran inside, grabbing change from my pocket and passing it toward the man behind the glass. I slipped in before the door shut and got on. I walked the steps to get to the top of the ferry and saw Mel looking off toward Dartmouth.

"Mel!" I ran up to her.

She turned, tears in her eyes, and looked surprised. "Adrian, what are you doin —"

"Are you okay?" I sat down, putting a hand on her shoulder. "I saw what happened."

"No." Mel wiped her eyes. "My dad . . . He just . . . I'm not okay, no."

"You don't have to be." I gave her a hug. "I just want you to be safe."

"Why do I have to fuck up everything?" she cried into my sweater while I held on to her.

"You know that's not true," I replied, resting my head on hers as night took over the sky.

★ ★ ★

As we left the Ferry terminal on the Dartmouth side, we were met with the train riding across the tracks. Mel stood there as it went by slowly.

"You ever just think about jumping on one of these things?" she asked with her head down. "To just get out of here."

"It gets more tempting every day," I told her, placing my hand in hers. We walked toward a bench facing the water and caught the view of Halifax.

"You must've heard what I said to my mom, huh?" Mel shrugged, looking across the water.

"I did," I replied, feeling awful about it. "She really just left because she wasn't ready?"

"I guess there's more to it. You know my dad, how

123

selfish he can be. He wanted Mom to dedicate her whole life to his business. Mom still wanted to go to school, try to get a degree, and she almost did."

"What happened?"

"I came into the equation." Mel looked down. "Having an unexpected child complicates things. So she put her dreams aside." I could see guilt cover Mel's face. "Going back to school turned into next year, then the year after, until she felt like she never could. She wanted to be more than a character in my father's story," Mel explained. "After the divorce, and dealing with a kid, she felt like she didn't have any breathing room."

I guess, in a way, I could see how Prisha felt trapped, but I also knew it must have been difficult for Mel to process.

"All she wanted to do is work in the arts. Not some stupid music shop. It was so hard for me to talk to her after she left." A tear rolled down Mel's cheek. "It always made me feel like I was too muc —"

"Mel, you're never too much." I squeezed her hand, wanting her to believe it. "You're everything anyone could ever ask for. You don't have to head home tonight. You can stay at my place."

"Thanks, AC," she said, taking a cigarette from her pocket. She looked at it for a minute, then shoved it back.

"Why'd you come over anyways?"

I knew it was going to be rough.

"I have to tell you something."

CHAPTER 11

Shoulders to Mountaintops

It was getting late. Mel and I were making our way back to my place. Mel parked her car over at Azra's and we walked the rest of the way to mine, mostly in silence. She walked ahead, when I just wanted her close. I was officially in my dream university program, and I felt awful. Maybe it was the timing of telling her? Or the disappointment of me no longer joining her on her tour? Last night we were having fun in the lake, calling it the centre of the universe, and now it felt like there was only distance between us.

"Are you upset about it?" I finally found the courage to ask.

"What?" She turned around, confused. "No. Of course not. I'm just thinking a lot."

"About what?"

"A lot," she replied quietly.

"Oh," I said. "It's okay if you're a little —"

"Adrian, please stop."

I did.

When we made it to my place, Mel wasn't really feeling like talking to anyone. That included my parents. We hopped on top of the green bin and managed to get to the window of my room. I just wanted to take her to a place where she felt safe and didn't have to think about the rest of the world.

"I'm proud of you," she told me, forcing a smile as I shut the window. "If that's what you were wondering."

"It's okay if you're sad about it." We both sat back on the bed.

"That just makes me sound selfish." She sighed.

I held onto her hand, and she held mine. Nobody ever told us how hard the summer between high school and university would be, or the decisions we'd have to make, or the goodbyes we'd have to say, or the distance it creates. Things were moving so fast, and I was afraid to let go. I wanted to be in the moment, instead of having it slip into a memory. I wanted to stay in the present, like a gift I wanted to keep. I didn't want her to be nostalgia. I just wanted her.

"Maybe we should talk." She sat up with her eyes closed.

"About . . . what?" I asked, frightened.

Before she could continue, I heard a voice from downstairs.

"He can't be serious. Why did he waste all of our time?" It was Dad.

"This has to be a mistake. We just went yesterday." Mom sounded defensive.

"Mistakes like this aren't just made. It says he dropped out of university."

I sat up quickly to see my laptop wasn't on my desk. *Goddamn fantasy football.*

"Shit." I got out of bed and peeked down the hall. I could see Mom and Dad's shadows on the wall.

"What's going on?" Mel asked.

"Nothing, I just have some explaining to do." I walked toward the stairs.

I could hear their voices go back and forth as I approached.

"Did you read this, too? He's in some eating disorder recovery group?" Dad said.

No. He's not supposed to know about that. Who does he think he is going on my laptop?

"Hey, come on now. That's his business. Not ours," Mom replied.

"It's a distraction, that's what it is. Kids today get too soft. Like that guys' group he's in."

"Why are you reading my blog posts and emails?" I showed my face as they stood by my laptop.

Dad caught eyes with me. "Why in the hell would you drop out?"

"I didn't drop —"

"We drove all the way up there!" Dad pointed at me. His face was red, and his gaze was looking through me, not at me. "I was getting ready to put a deposit on your dorm, and you go and do this?"

"I'm still goi —"

"Why would you drop out? For what? Do you know

127

how much I've been saving up for you? I wanted you to focus!" He raised his voice. I felt my throat tighten. I almost didn't want to speak. "What do you plan to do? Stay in your room all year?"

"Let him explain," Mom said, seeing my reaction.

"Let me guess, you wanna go with Mel on some trip? You have to learn it's time to grow up. I know you love that girl, but it's a stupid idea." He raised his hands, then slammed them on the table.

"You might wanna stop talking," I suggested. *Mel can't hear this. Not now.*

"You might wanna start taking this seriously!" he yelled over me. "You don't wanna end up like some loser!"

I'd never heard Dad sound so disappointed before. It reminded me of all the times I felt like I let him down. I hated that he said that. I hated how he made me feel like a kid, and what I hated most was that Mel heard it all. When I turned to my right, she was standing in the stairway.

"Mel?" My dad was shocked to see her.

"Don't worry about it, Mr. Carter." Mel shrugged, forcing a half-grin. "I've had a lot of people tell me that exact thing this week."

"Oh, Melody. He didn't mean it." Mom tried to comfort her. Mel stepped away as a look of guilt crept over my dad's face.

"Mel, wait —" I tried to say something, anything.

"Don't worry about it, Adrian. It sounds like you have a lot going on. I'll see you around." She turned, wiping her eyes. I tried to go after her, but Mom stopped me.

"Just let her go," she said. "She needs space."

"What the hell is wrong with you?" My gaze whipped over to Dad.

"Adrian, I —"

"Shut the fuck up!" *I don't know where that came from.* "I got accepted into community studies and made the switch, big fucking deal!" I pointed at him. "If you paid attention to me once in the past three years, you'd know this is what I want to do. You'd know how much working with the guys' group means to me, and you'd know how important it is for me to help young people with eating disorders."

"You need to grow up and take responsibility."

"Just like how you took responsibility? I'm not you! I'm smart enough not to make the same mistakes you did. I'm smart enough not to lose this scholarship!" I shouted.

Dad didn't see that coming. There was a look of embarrassment on his face, but he fought through it, took a breath and said, "A program like that would only keep you in the past, just like those lessons you do at the library. Stop letting that nonsense hold you back!"

"What held you back, huh? You said yourself the walls in the house are thin, and when I needed you, you chose to be a coward!" I went off. "You wanna know why this is important to me? It's important to me because a lot of these teenagers who struggle have fathers like you!"

Dad's eyes widened and there was a silence between us that wasn't going anywhere. I knew I hurt him. I wanted to. I'd said what I needed to say, so I took my laptop and readied to leave the room.

"Adrian?" Mom tried to grab my hand.

"He needed to hear it," I said. "Dad, if I'm being

completely honest, I was better off before you decided to be present."

I was glad I'd finally stood up for myself and for Mel. It wasn't the way I wanted to tell my parents about my plan, but it was finally out in the open. I didn't want Mel to have heard what Dad said, but she did. When I got upstairs, I sent her a message.

Me: Mel, I'm so sorry. Do you wanna come back?
Mel: Just give me some space, okay?

I laid back on my bed and threw my phone across the room.

Dad had no right to raise his voice to me. He made me feel tiny and worthless. I slumped out of bed, and picked my phone back up, scrolling through my contacts seeing who I could chat with. I knew one person who'd be up for a late-night coffee.

★ ★ ★

"Wow, so you really got into it with everyone, huh?" Azra asked, sipping on a mocha.

I trusted Azra a lot. She always knew the right thing to say, and how to go about it. We were at Redemption House Cafe, sitting up on the second floor with no one around. I told her the complete story, what I said to Prisha, Martin and my Dad. How Mel walked in and then ran off. I went from being accepted into my dream university program to having the worst night of my life.

"Yeah." I placed my head down on the table. "To top it all off, I'm supposed to give a presentation tomorrow, and I'm so not ready," I vented. The last thing I wanted to do was let Bobby down, especially on our last session of the summer.

"Adrian, can I ask you a question?"

"Go for it." I sat back up and crossed my arms.

"What kind of person are you trying to become? You're so wrapped up in everyone else's expectations that you can barely find your own path," Azra said. "I know it's not easy. Parents are rough. Heck, my parents think this tour is a terrible idea." She laughed. "That doesn't mean I'm not going to fight for it. Because I want it, so, so badly. What happened with your dad wasn't cool, but is this future something worth fighting for?"

"Yes," I said without hesitation. "Absolutely."

"Then what's stopping you?"

"Myself." I shook my head. "I feel like I can't own the things I've been through, because the one person who was supposed to be there for me was complicit in it. How can I teach a group of teenagers about eating disorders when my dad thinks it's weak of me to even talk about? He found out about my recovery group and told me I need to move on. Now I feel like I have to wait for some kind of permission that I know isn't going to come."

"I'm so sorry that happened to you, Adrian." Azra patted my back. "You deserved support. Now look at you, you're draining yourself out just trying to become all the things you needed from other people."

She was right. It was like I needed to spell it out for it to make sense. "I guess that's part of the reason I fight so hard for the teenagers in my recovery group, so they don't have to go through what I did. If Dad doesn't respect that, it means he doesn't respect me." I sat back to see the night sky out the window. It had been the only calming thing from the storm of a day.

"You know," Azra said, "people always used to make fun of me, or snicker about me being different in the punk scene." She pointed to her hijab. "But I never let it stop me, because my passion mattered more than what others thought about me. When things got rough, my dad used to always tell me, if you wear your heart on your sleeve, don't let this world make you roll up your heartbeat." She smiled. "In other words, never let anyone change you, because that permission you're waiting for is never going to come. This is your story, so stop letting other people tell it for you."

Dad kept telling me I needed to move on, but that wasn't always an option. I couldn't move on without owning my past.

"You're right, this is my story to tell, on my terms. Thanks, Azra."

"That's what friends are for." Azra pulled me in for a hug. "FYI, Mel needs space. She picked up her car in a rush earlier. She'll talk to you when she's ready. In the meantime, you got some work to do. So I suggest you get back to your place, and prep for that killer presentation."

CHAPTER 12

Honesty and the Baggage That Comes Along With It

"Eating disorders can impact anyone, but they're treatable."
I stood with a clicker in my hand. The projector showed
a diagram of how eating disorders affect Canadians. It was
the last session of the summer, and as Bobby promised, it
was my turn to lead the group. I didn't get much sleep.
Instead, I stayed up working on a PowerPoint that nobody
was paying attention to.

"You got this," Bobby whispered. The boys around us
had their eyes all over the room, snickering at one another, not giving me any attention.

I was nervous and honestly woke up that morning not
feeling too great. I couldn't stop thinking about Mel, or
the argument I had with Dad.

"An eating disorder is a term that can be used to de-
scribe anything from binge eating, to bulimia, to anorexia,"

I told the group. Lenny yawned, catching everyone's attention. I ignored it and kept going.

"The reason I wanted to talk about this today is because we often don't hear male perspectives around eating disorders, and I can assure you they are pretty common. I was reading a study that —"

I was interrupted by Isaac watching TikToks on his phone, which made some of the other guys around him to take a peek.

"C'mon, guys, Adrian is working hard here!" Bobby raised his voice. It didn't calm any of them down though. I just stood there, feeling stupid for even trying to talk to these guys about eating disorders and recovery. None of them cared. If anything, they were just showing me it didn't matter, the things I'd been through didn't matter, and the . . .

"The work you do matters." I remembered what Mel had told me as I shut my eyes. Sometimes it didn't feel that way. Sometimes it felt thankless. More than sometimes, actually.

I couldn't stop thinking about what Dad said, about just burying my past inside me and moving forward. It had been weighing on me. I didn't want to live my life that way. I wanted to live in a world like Azra said: a world where I could wear my heart on my sleeve and not roll up my heartbeat. I wanted to love myself for who I was, not what I did. That started with owning my story, and not being ashamed of what I'd been through. I just needed to . . .

Be brave.

"I was sixteen years old the first time I purged." I spoke loud enough that the guys in the group turned toward me. "I remember what I thought before I did it. 'Do I really wanna be one of those kids? This isn't a boy thing.' But I thought it would help me," I said as I powered down the projector. There was no point in continuing the presentation.

"Soon after, I started to notice the little things. I could fit into a shirt that was a size smaller. People weren't as rude to me about my appearance. Heck, I even began getting compliments. Sure, I did kickboxing on the side, though to be honest, I just used it as a way to make it seem like I took a healthy route. The truth is, I didn't. It was a lie I held onto. Part of the reason being, it was the first time my dad ever told me he was proud of me," I said it out loud and it kind of felt like a weight had been lifted. Everyone looked in my direction with a supportive presence, and I felt comfortable enough to continue.

"It wasn't until later that bad stuff started to happen. My hair began thinning. I felt like I was going to pass out most of the time. I was always starving. I lost a lot of the people I held close, and it made me realize the weight of my decisions. If you're wondering what I do outside this group, I work with other teens who have eating disorders, so they don't have to go through what I did. And today, for our last session, I wanted to be brave," I told them. "A lot of us feel we have to bury the most vulnerable parts of ourselves to move forward. It's not true. I think for a lot of guys, we feel we can't be open and vulnerable. Heck, I just got into a fight with my dad about this last night."

"Wait, why'd you get into a fight with your dad about this?" Lenny asked. I could hear the regret in his voice.

"We got into a fight because I told him I wanted to go to school for a program called community studies, to work with young folks like you, and teens who are like me. When I went through everything, I was mostly on my own. I didn't have many folks to look up to."

"I look up to you . . ." Isaac said, turning his phone off. "Maybe Bobby was right. Sometimes we don't always know who's in the room. This stuff is important, and hearing about it matters."

I felt like I could finally let go of the breath that was trapped inside of my chest. For so long, I ran away from things that were supposed to be buried deep inside, and that day, I decided to change that. Maybe I couldn't solve all the problems, but I could, at the very least, try to become the person I needed. For people who were like me.

★ ★ ★

"Adrian, you facilitated that like a champ!" Bobby gave me a pat on the back as the teenagers were leaving. "Gosh, that university has no idea how lucky they are to have someone like you. When you spoke, reclaimed that space, you could hear a pin drop. How the hell am I supposed to replace you?"

"I'm sure someone will rise to the occasion, Bobby." I smiled, patting his back too.

"Y'know, I, uh, don't know too much about your dad, but he should be extremely proud of having a son like you.

"If you ever need a letter of reference, anything like that, you have my number, kid."

"Thanks, Bobby," I replied, packing up. "I'll be in touch."

The weight had officially been lifted from my shoulders, and some of my anxiety drifted away. I knew the feeling was temporary. I still let myself bask in it for the time being. As I walked outside, I looked at the community board and saw a poster that read: HARBOR GIRLS VS BROWN, BLACK & INFAMOUS, BATTLE OF THE BANDS FINALE.

I was curious how the other competition went, and I wondered how Kara felt about battling her old band. Heck, she was gonna kill it.

★ ★ ★

When I got home, I walked into the kitchen and saw Dad sat at the table, eating. He looked away when he realized it was me. Typical.

I stepped outside to the back deck and saw Mom pulling clothes from the line and throwing them in a laundry basket.

"She doing okay?" Mom asked without looking at me.

"Who?" I asked, then instantly regretted it. "Oh. I don't know. I haven't heard from her today."

"You plan on checking in?"

"I do. I'm just . . . not exactly over what happened last night." I sat at the patio table.

"You and your father really got into it," Mom acknowledged, taking a seat beside me. "You know, Adrian, your dad should have listened to what you had to say before acting like a fool."

I was glad Mom saw it that way. I didn't think I could handle having both of them upset at me.

Mom looked at me, her face full of sorrow. "Adrian, I never knew you were in an eating disorder recovery group," she said. "I didn't even know you had an eating disorder. Not until your father started talking about it, and honestly, it makes sense. You lost weight really fast, faster than you should have. I should have noticed."

I lost weight way too fast, because I couldn't stop purging. I used to hate so many parts of myself. Sometimes it was based in anger, in sadness and a lot of it was because of guilt. We were never a rich family growing up. Mom spent a lot of time finding hand-me-downs from older cousins, but they never fit me right. I knew about the times my parents stressed over money, and worried about the clothes I needed because I was a bigger size. It didn't exactly make me love myself. I knew they wished I wasn't so big, even if they didn't say it. So yeah, there were parts of myself I hated. It always came back to my body. But I never wanted Mom to think anything else other than I was fine.

"I'm sorry I wasn't there for you when —"

"No," I cut her off. "Mom, this isn't your fault. This is a secret I chose to keep. This is —"

"Something your father was complicit in, and something I fell into too."

"It's not about that. It's about me choosing to be —"

"The person you needed when you were younger. I get it. You made yourself clear. I'm proud of you for doing this, but I need you to listen." Mom's eyes gazed into mine. "Honesty is a beautiful thing when you find the courage to own your past. Just understand that there is baggage which comes along with it. I might not have known about it, but that doesn't mean I shouldn't have. I'm not faulting you for choosing not to tell me. I'm just saying I can't help feeling guilty over it. You're my boy, and I should have been there."

I never wanted that to happen. I never wanted Mom to carry the weight of it.

"When it comes to raising kids, I remember buying so many of those silly books thinking it'd help. But once things get moving, you're better off throwing all that out the window. Being a parent is hard. You're always worrying about the big things. What if something awful happens? Where are we going to get the money? What are we going to do? We forget to do the simplest things, like just checking in. You were always a good kid, so we never thought we had to worry. Now I know the subtle pressure I put on you about your weight impacted you. I never meant to hurt you." Her eyes began to water. "Adrian, I'm sorry."

I pulled Mom into a hug and squeezed tight.

"The biggest fear we have as parents is failure. Believe it or not, your father feared that too."

"He has a funny way of showing it." I let go.

"He's not perfect, I know that. Just know he's trying. Give him time. He heard your honesty, and right now, he's ruffling through the baggage."

I took what Mom said to me about honesty and thought it'd be important to bring up in my last blog post. It was that unfortunate time of the summer when I had to shift gears and let them know I was leaving. That evening, I sat at my desk, opened my laptop and began typing:

Honesty & the Baggage That Comes Along With It
Hey, y'all. It's Adrian here. I wanted to take some time to talk and let everyone know, as things slow down and we get closer to the horrible reality that summer doesn't last forever, that this will be my last blog post. As some of you may know, I'm about to venture off into the world of academia in a few short weeks. I'm going through a lot of changes. I'm going to be moving up to Cape Breton with my best friend. I'll be a student in a program called community studies to pursue a passion that I love. But for everything I'm excited about, there's a lot I'm fearful of too. Mostly, the idea of saying goodbye to the people I love. Not just my parents, I'll miss my community of friends who I hold close. From my unpacking masculinity group, to my friend Bobby, Azra, Jade, Kara and . . . my girlfriend. There's a silver lining to everything in life, and even the best decisions you make come with baggage you're not always prepared to deal with. My last piece of advice I want you all to know in here is this: Trust the people around you. Even if they sometimes feel like they're worlds away, they're still close enough to your orbit to be present.
　　Be Honest. Be Brave. Be You.
　　It was a pleasure being part of your journey,
　　With gratitude,
　　Adrian

I hit enter, sat back in my chair and got a nice view of the moon outside my window. I knew Mel was somewhere under that moon too, and it was about time I checked in. As I picked up my phone, I noticed I already received a text from her fifteen minutes ago.

Mel: Adrian, I think we should talk.

CHAPTER 13

The Future and Other Terrifying Scenarios

I made my way toward the school. Walking toward your high school feels different after you graduate. I had a feeling this was going to be the last time for a while. I got to the fire escape started climbing the ladder to the roof.

This rooftop was the first place I told Mel I liked her when we were both freshmen. I remember being so scared, telling her that "I liked her a lot . . . and stuff," then shying away from eye contact. I'd been fearful I ruined something great, and wished I never said anything. Then all I remember is her lifting my chin and meeting me halfway. Her lips met mine, and I closed my eyes. Anxiety made its way out of my chest and was replaced with a warmth that felt like magic. I had no idea the best was yet to come.

That nostalgia filled my heart as I made it to the top. The difference between then and now is that the love was still there, but I could feel anxiety creeping its way back in.

I could see her in the distance.

"Mel?" I headed toward her. Her back was turned as she sat on the edge, looking off toward the commons.

"Hey, Adrian." She turned to look at me. "I think we should talk."

She got to her feet and stepped toward me. I could tell she didn't want a hug, or anything physical.

"Mel, I'm sorry you heard what you did. My dad is kind of an idiot sometimes. What he said isn't true."

Her arms were crossed, and she wasn't making eye contact. Something inside of her was conflicted. She took a breath and said, "It's not what he said that made me leave. Adrian, I've had people tell me my dreams were stupid. It's nothing new."

The sad part about it was I knew she wasn't lying.

"I, uh . . . I wanted to talk about the future, and other terrifying scenarios."

"Mel, we don't have to do this tonight."

"We do." She looked up at me. "Finals is in two weeks. I'm going to fight like hell. I'm going to fight for the times I never stood up for myself. I'm going to fight for my dreams. I'm going to fight for a future that I want."

She deserved to fight for everything she wanted.

"The future that I want, Adrian, involves you."

There it is. That's why she wanted to talk.

"Mel, I want you in my future, too. But I'm moving in two weeks."

"Hear me out." She pulled my arm. "Imagine all the places we could go. If we win, we're going to start off in

Montreal. It's beautiful there. I want you to experience the music scene, then we'd head off to Ottawa. We can get pictures at Parliament, then find the Museum of Natural History." She sounded nervous. "Then Toronto. Me and you can get a picture in the CN Tower. There'll be other places, like Winnipeg, Vancouver . . ."

That was her dream. She'd been fighting for something like this ever since she started her band. I've been her biggest supporter. With that being said, I had to be honest and find the courage to say it wasn't my dream.

"Mel, this sounds really great. It does. It's just . . . I have a responsibility now." It hurt for me to say.

"Is this what you want to do? You can wait a year if you want. Forget about this scholarship and stop trying to live up to these expectations."

"It's not that easy," I said. "Mel, I know this has never been an easy place for either of us, and even if it's hard, this is still my home. I wanna try to make it better."

"Make it better for who?" she cut in. "This place doesn't deserve someone like you. Your dad going off like that, those kids not realizing how important you are, you're trying to make this a better place for anybody that isn't you."

"That's not true. I opened up today. I finally told them my story during my presentation. I was scared, and I knew I had to be brave. They absorbed it, Mel. They —"

"Probably only listened because they had to," she interrupted.

That was hurtful. She'd never been to any of those sessions before, she didn't know.

"Kids are insensitive, rude and . . ."

"Learning, growing and sometimes they listen." I pulled my arm back. "Mel, this work matters. You even said it."

"You have me, Kara, Azra, Jade. We appreciate you, and we're going to make the best of it. What else do you want?"

I loved all of them deeply. For the past few years, they were who I turned to when I needed support. That's what made it harder, because I had to make the change. *For me.*

"Mel, we can still make this work. You won't be on your tour forever, only a few months. I'm sure we can figure it out. I can always get the Maritime Bus and come back to the city to visit."

"Adrian," Mel tried to cut me off.

"University isn't going to be forever. I'm still gonna be active in Halifax and —"

"Listen."

"It'll be the holidays before you know it and —"

"I'm not coming back!" Her voice cut through mine like a knife. My heart went on pause. *She isn't coming back? What does she mean?*

"You're not . . . what?" I was struggling to catch my shaky voice.

"If we win in two weeks, that's my ticket out of this place," Mel responded, biting her lip.

"I was just talking to Azra last night. She never mentioned —"

"She doesn't know. None of them do." Mel's voice cracked under the pressure. "I'm telling them at our next practice. I don't know if they'll want to stay with me or come home. Regardless, this is something I gotta do. For me."

My heart felt like it was crashing down. I knew how hard this had been for her, I didn't want to think what life would be like if she was just . . . gone.

"So . . . where does that leave us?"

Mel let out a breath, trying to catch her voice before the tears took it away. She placed her palms on my cheeks, and no matter how hard I tried, I couldn't shy away. I basked in the warmth of her hands. "I never planned on coming back . . ." I could hear the regret in her voice. She closed her eyes while the tears rolled down her face.

"Mel?" I stepped away. "You wanted me to go with you, apply for community studies, you wanted to . . ."

That's when it finally made sense.

"You wanted to convince me to not go to university, didn't you?"

"I . . . I thought maybe we could start new. Somewhere else, y'know? I thought we could cut the baggage here. Find someplace safe for the both of us." She looked away.

"You knew I wanted to come back." I couldn't believe what I was hearing. "You knew I wanted to go to school."

"And maybe you can. There are a million other universities out there. We could find a place where you're not harassed by security or cops all the time."

"I don't think a change in location would stop that." I was shocked. I was so disappointed in her. "Why are you just telling me this now? I thought you were happy for me. You said yourself that you wanted me to do this."

"Things change, okay!"

Everything got silent. Mel never raised her voice like that to me, and it felt so off. It put me on edge.

"Why don't you just let go of this place!" she demanded. "This city never did anything for us. It's the cause of what went wrong. Why won't you just come with me?"

"Because I'm not running away from my problems!" I snapped and instantly regretted it.

She caught her breath and stood tense, facing me.

"Is that what you think this is?" She looked like she'd been struck.

"Mel, I didn't mean it like that." I backed away.

"I heard you loud and clear, okay." She lowered her voice. "Even if your dad is an asshole, you always had him, Adrian. You always had both your parents and a community who accepted you. Don't imply that I'm running away from something I never had. I had to fight for everything I have, and I thought you would understand that. I thought you would understand that I don't wanna fight anymore."

She felt more distant than ever before. I shut my eyes, wishing the roof of the school would swallow me.

"You know," she spoke softly. "This summer between us is getting closer to the end."

"What are you saying?" I opened my eyes.

"I'm saying . . ." She took a long breath. "That I need you to be good to yourself. Even if that doesn't include me."

"Mel, don't do this." I reached out to her.

"We all knew it was bound to happen." She stepped away. "That's how this goes. I find people who care about me. They leave. The cycle repeats and I'm alone." She took another deep breath and let it out. "And this is the part where you go to university, make your family proud, make your community proud and become the person the world needs. You have time, and you're really lucky. Goodbye, Adrian."

She walked away toward the ladder. I didn't chase her. I wish I did. I felt so empty, so awful. She wanted me there with her so badly and I couldn't be. It hurt so bad. Tears began rolling down my cheeks, and I kept thinking back to the night a few summers ago. I was so scared to tell Mel I liked her on that same rooftop, the same one I was now sitting on alone. I worried I'd ruined something great, with no idea that the best days were ahead of us. And when the magic faded, I could hear the music stop. The rest of my world went silent. I thought our track list was infinite, but every song eventually ends. Even the ones that are your favourites.

CHAPTER 14
Finals Night

For the next two weeks, I rarely left my bed. My parents felt awful about me and Mel breaking up, so they gave me space.

I didn't sleep, talk to many friends or even shower too often. I found comfort in old habits though. I binge ate whatever I could get my hands on. An empty ice cream container and a box of granola bars could be found on my nightstand. I was spiralling, and I felt pathetic because of it.

I heard a knock while I was covered in blankets.

"Adrian?" My door opened slightly. It was Mom, and she slipped inside. "Adrian, can we talk?"

"You're already in here," I said, not facing her. I was heading off to Cape Breton the next morning. The belongings I was bringing were already packed away, so I guess I was just waiting.

Mom took a seat in the chair by my desk.

"Your father was thinking about going to dinner tonight, y'know. Just the three of us."

"It sounds like that'd be just one long awkward silence." I turned over.

"Yeah . . ." Mom replied. "But that's not why I told him it was a bad idea."

Huh? I was surprised Mom didn't want to go through with it.

"Adrian, we feel awful about what happened with you and Mel."

"What Dad said didn't exactly help. Maybe he can take a lesson in responding instead of reacting." I sat up.

"Honestly, you're right," Mom agreed. "Adrian, we're both sorry about that. If we could take it back, we would."

"Then where's Dad? How come he can't apologize?"

"He'll come around in time. Trust me," Mom tried to reassure me. "But about tonight, you know it's Mel's show, right?"

I did. I was surprised Mom knew about it. It was the night Brown, Black & Infamous was facing off against Harbor Girls.

"Yeah, what's your point? Thought you didn't care about that."

"That was your father who said that. I always thought Mel's band was . . . pretty badass." I was surprised Mom said badass. "I know that's where you want to be."

"What? No. Mel broke up with me. I know the last person she'd want to see is me."

"That's not true, and you know it," Mom said. "You and her share so much history. You already know I love that girl. I hate what your father said just as much as you do. That girl is special, and I knew it from the moment your eyes lit up when she came over here the first time."

"My eyes never lit up." I tried hiding my grin.

"Yes, Adrian. Yes, they did." Mom threw my lies out the window. "I love the way she treated my boy." She moved to sit on the side of my bed. "And how she brought out the best in you. You two went through your ups and downs, and that taught you so much. It made you grow into the man you are. When you two started dating, I was scared I'd lose you."

"Lose me?" I asked. "How?"

"Because you were growing up too fast," Mom whispered. "If I could, I'd want you to stay my boy just a little longer." She played with my hair. "At some point, you see your boy make changes, not only for himself, but also for the people around him. You watch him fall in love, and feel good knowing there's someone out there for him."

The hardest part of growing up was knowing those three years would only be Polaroids to look back on.

"I guess if you're lucky enough to know what love feels like, there's a chance you probably know what heartbreak is too," I sighed.

"You're wise." Mom smiled. "Heartbreak doesn't mean you gotta give up the friendship. It doesn't mean you still can't show her support. I don't know the full extent of what Mel's going through with her parents. What I do know is that they don't know her worth."

I guess we both agreed on that. I thought about going. It would be the last opportunity I'd have to see them perform. Mel worked really hard to get the band to where they were, and they were going to tear it up.

Mom looked into my eyes and said, "Take the rest of the time you have, and you go say goodbye. She might not have said it, but believe me when I tell you she needs your support right now." Mom kissed my forehead. "I'm going to miss my boy. I'm sure she's going to miss hers too."

When Mom left, I lurked the Facebook event page. It was labelled: Brown, Black & Infamous vs. 3AM: Finals Night.

3AM? That was the band Donny made fun of the night of the first round. I thought Mel's band would face off against Harbor Girls. I called Donny's cell.

"Donny," I said when he picked up. "Mel's facing off against 3AM tonight?"

"Yeah, bad news," Donny admitted. "Harbor Girls broke up."

"Then shouldn't Brown, Black & Infamous win by forfeit?"

"Not exactly," Donny explained. "The response was that the funders need a second show to happen before distributing funds. Word on the street is, the organizers feel 3AM would pull more revenue to the show anyways, so they offered them a spot."

"No." I was getting angry. "3AM has twice the number of followers than Brown, Black & Infamous." I looked over their Instagram page. They had over 5,000 followers.

"It's an unjust world." Donny sighed in defeat.

"No, this isn't going to happen," I vented. "They aren't doing another competition where these girls get sidelined by basic white dudes!" I was trying to think of ways we could get the community to show up. I only had 503 friends on Facebook and even then only two might show up if I asked. I went down my profile to see what groups I was in and noticed the BIPOC Graduating Classes of HRM. I clicked on the link and saw it was students of colour from Halifax West, to Dartmouth High, to Citadel, to Prince Andrew High. It had over 1,500 members.

"Is Shay the only admin of the BIPOC graduate group?"

"Ha," Donny laughed. "Is that even a question?"

I looked down the admin page and saw Shay's profile. "Dammit."

Those organizers were scum. They knew 3AM would bring fanboys from here to Bedford. Even if Brown, Black & Infamous had their fan base, it might not be enough. We needed help from our peers, from others who had a similar experience to us. We needed . . .

"Adrian," Donny laughed. "I was on Shay's laptop, and you really don't think I searched for his passwords?"

"Donny . . . you're still an asshole for doing that." I smiled. "Send them to me."

"You got it."

A few moments later, a message from Donny showed up:

Password:ForTheDreamers@902

I logged in and felt anxious as hell.

"The floor is yours," Donny told me. "One way or another, I'll see you tonight."

I sat in front of my webcam, and hit the live button: The camera opened up and I could see myself on the screen. Everyone in the group received a notification saying I started a live video. I really should have shaved first. But I knew what I had to do. Fight for Mel.

"Hey, everyone," was all I said before I felt the pressure. They were starting to tune in. "My name is Adrian Carter. I'm sure some of you know me from Citadel. I wear a lot of different hats. Some of you know me as the big kid who lost weight. Some of you know me from working at the library. Some of you know me as just the quiet guy." The views were coming in: five, then up to fifteen, then twenty.

"Well, tonight, I have something to say. There's an event going on over at the warehouses in Burnside. It's finals night for a competition called the Maritime Indie Battle of the Bands. Not a great title, I know."

102, 123, 140.

"For the past two years, myself, and a group of badass, racialized punks have been to these shows. Unfortunately, not always with open arms. Being Brown, being Black, in these spaces always creates an environment where we don't always feel welcomed," I explained. "I've felt first-hand what this looks like."

200, 204, 205.

"I've had people trying to grab my hair. I was accused of stealing posters from the merch table. I'm always asked if I'm 'the guy'. If you don't know what that means, it means drug dealer. I think."

382, 390.

"I've seen voices be silenced, especially the ones who need to be heard." I was sad at the truth. "Today I'm witnessing systematic issues where an organization plans to silence women of colour for profit." I felt angry knowing this was what they were doing. "Tonight, I need your help."

400, 468, 500.

"We need to take a stand and let them know we don't roll like that. That we deserve to be in these spaces without harassment or assumptions. We deserve an equal opportunity to be heard. They can't keep pushing us out. So tonight, if you're down to come out to a punk show, let's support a group of women who have worked so hard to get to where they're at, and stop some out of touch organizers from taking it away," I said. "Brown, Black & Infamous is a promise to not apologize for your presence. It's about being unapologetic in our skin. To be proud of who we are and own the parts of ourselves people try to shame us for.

"This band is a promise to not let this world damper our magic or take away the strength in our identities. I'm tired of people telling us otherwise. I'm sure you are too. We are so much more than the stereotypes others come up with in their heads. We all have stories that deserve to shine." I smiled bravely. "So tonight. Let's be unapologetically loud. Let's be Brown, let's be Black, and let's be Infamous." I hit the stop button and noticed we'd made it to 723 views.

"This might work," I said as I caught my breath.

★ ★ ★

The address on the poster brought me to an abandoned warehouse in Burnside. Getting the bus there wasn't the greatest, but I could hear loud music from a distance, so I knew I was in the right place. I saw cars, vans and trucks parked outside with people sitting on hoods, drinking and smoking weed. I stepped to the entrance and noticed a large man in a jean vest with a Mohawk.

"Twenty bucks to get in," was all he said.

I guess I didn't get the VIP treatment anymore. I emptied my pocket and gave him the bills and change I had, knowing I'd be walking home.

Inside, red lights and loud music filled the room. I could see albums, posters and CDs from Brown, Black & Infamous and 3AM over at the merchandise table. Of course, 3AM had three times the amount of merch, and more money in the jar.

I frowned, then heard a voice echo through the warehouse. "All right, tonight is the night, two bands, one winner, a national tour is on the line and it is up to YOU! The crowd! To decide who's representing us!" The host energized the crowd. He was wearing an orange beanie with the same crusty overalls from round one that needed to be washed. "We got a band of unapologetic, racialized punks going against west end misfits. Tonight we have Brown, Black & Infamous going against 3AM!" The crowd erupted again, sending a shockwave through the warehouse.

"Brown, Black & Infamous, you're on deck. 3AM, the floor is yours!"

Chet and three other white dudes stormed the stage; they began thrashing away while the crowd formed into a mosh pit. Moshing wasn't my thing, so I went back to the parking lot. I was so nervous. I had no idea if my plan would work, and I felt like I was going to vomit.

That's when I heard my name.

"Adrian!" I looked over to see Donny with the widest smile I'd ever seen on him.

"Donny, you're here." I gave him props, realizing he wore a green t-shirt saying Dude Bro Number 1.

"Nice touch," I noted.

"I'm not the only one. Follow me." He grabbed my shoulder and took me around the side of the building.

When we made it out, I turned to see a large group of what had to be at least fifty people hanging outside of the warehouse.

"Look at this spur-of-the-moment activism, or social justice. Whatever Mel calls it." Donny grinned.

A line of Black and Brown punks were chatting, hyping themselves up. Some of them had home-made Brown, Black & Infamous shirts.

"The community . . . showed up." I smiled.

"What's up, everybody!" Donny yelled, getting everyone's attention. "Who's ready to take up some space!"

"Let's make some noise for 3AM!" I heard the host's voice inside the venue. A lot of the crowd cheered. Not us though. We stayed silent, saving our energy. I couldn't believe we were actually doing this.

"Now, let's make some noise for Brown, Black & Infamous!" the host yelled.

"That's our cue!" Donny yelled, and everyone stormed the venue, making their way to the front of the crowd. I was right in there giggling with them. There was a rhythm, and we were raising the roof, chanting.

"Brown, Black and Infamous! Brown, Black and Infamous! Brown, Black and Infamous!"

I watched all four girls walk onto the stage. I could sense the intensity from far away. Mel went up to the microphone while Azra went behind her drum set, Kara and

157

Jade both holding their guitars. I put up my hood, hoping Mel wouldn't see me. I wanted to be there to support her, not to be a distraction.

Mel's eyes widened when she saw everyone front and centre. She looked amazed, taking in the moment. "Holy shit. Let's knock this fucking warehouse down!" she screamed and started playing her guitar while Azra kept up from behind. Jade kicked in with the bassline and Kara went in with the lead shortly after.

Kara was tearing it up, and the crowd was loving it. There were so many melanated hands in the air, unapologetically taking up space at the front of the stage. Azra took over with a drum solo and I rocked my head back and forth with the crowd.

Mel moved to the microphone and began singing.

"Show me healing/Show me love/Take me as I am."

She sang those lyrics truthfully, and so did we. All of us screaming the lyrics back as loud as we could. The rest of the band went silent while Mel thrashed her guitar, showing the world what she really was, a song that everyone needed to hear.

She stopped singing, but the audience still sang the lyrics back. She kept strumming her guitar along with the collective voices. Jade, Azra and Kara clearly weren't expecting that response, and Mel smiled for the first time in a while. Her strumming eventually faded away. The audience erupted into noise that shook the entire warehouse.

"I didn't mean in a literal sense, guys!" Mel couldn't contain her grin. "Thank you!"

She stepped back, and the host took the mic.

"All right, all right, it's that time of night!" the host yelled. "3AM, get up here!"

The white boys returned looking shook. I would be too.

"You know the drill. If you vote 3AM, make some noise!"

The crowd in the back cheered, but most of us in the front stayed silent. I was scared. This was the moment we'd been waiting for all summer. It came down to this: we had to be loud. I shut my eyes, feeling lost in the noise. I wanted this for Mel. *I want this for her so badly.*

"Now, Brown, Black & Infamous!"

I opened my eyes and yelled at the top of my lungs, jumping up and down with all the other Black and Brown folks in the front. My hood fell off in the excitement. The noise echoed so loud that it felt like it lifted the entire warehouse from the ground. It wasn't slowing down.

"We have it!" the host cut through the noise. "The winner of the Maritime Indie Battle of the Bands goes to Brown, Black & Infamous!"

Mel's eyes widened and her jaw dropped. Everyone around us cheered, and the girls in the back all pulled her into a hug.

I guess Mel really was going on the journey she'd been waiting for. I couldn't help but smile. When she let go of her bandmates, it was like there was a magnet between us. She caught eyes with me. She stared for a minute and began walking toward me until the host and other organizers started talking to her.

"Mel, you got some CDs to sign, and we need some info for the grant your band is getting," I managed to hear the host say.

I knew she had business to take care of, and I didn't want to get into the middle of it. I was just glad she won. I backed away, going out the way I came and made my way into the night.

CHAPTER 15
Worthy of Love

When I got home that night, everything finally kicked in. I assumed my parents were asleep, so I made my way to my room. Walking home from Burnside should have been tiring, but I was wide awake. I opened the door to my bedroom to see everything packed up in boxes. I knew what I was taking and what I was leaving behind. I guess I was finally ready for a new beginning. The hardest part about a new beginning means there's an end too. Those thoughts filled my head as I looked over at my desk to see the picture of me and Mel at prom. It was the photo we took while we were lying in the grass beneath the stars. I left it where it was, and took a moment to see those stars through my window.

I knew those stars would always stay in place, and no matter where I went, even if I wanted to move on, she'd be somewhere beneath them too. I remembered what she said, about the centre of the universe being wherever we met.

I took off my sweater and jeans and laid back in boxers and a t-shirt. I wondered if Donny felt what I was feeling. At least we'd be in it together. I should have waited to see if he'd give me a lift. I guess I just wanted to be alone. Spending five hours on the road with Donny the next morning would be enough.

Mel and the band must have felt on top of the world. They deserved all the praise they got. I'm glad Mom told me to go to the show. I wouldn't have otherwise.

I closed my eyes, hoping to finally get some rest. Instead, sleep was interrupted by a loud thud on my window.

"Holy shit!" I almost fell out of my bed.

I got up to see a shadow at my window. I began to freak out as I watched fingers climb beneath it, opening it up.

"Adrian, it's only me," I heard a familiar voice. *It's her.*

"Mel? What are you doing here?" I asked. "You just won the biggest competition of your life."

She didn't respond right away. Instead, she looked out the window and grabbed her box of cigarettes, before she pulled out a smoke. She shook her head and threw the entire box out the window.

"You know my parents will think those are mine, right?"

"Then I'll clean it up on the way out." She looked back. I couldn't see her face, but her silhouette told me she was hurting. Her shoulders were tense, and her head was down.

"Do you wanna sit down? Can I get you some water?" I asked.

"No. I don't know." She shook her head. "I don't even know why I came here. I just . . . I just want to talk."

"Of course."

"I didn't expect you to show up tonight." Mel leaned against the wall. "Mom, Dad, no one close to me came."

"I'm sorry they didn't."

I saw her take a breath and cross her arms. "Donny told me what you did. Why?"

"Because it's important to you. You're important."

Mel looked back out my window. I could see the moonlight splash against her face. She looked tired. So, so tired.

"Adrian . . . you were the first person who ever accepted me for who I am. You never tried to change me. You never told me to be different. There was never a standard, there was never conditional love. You always seen me, for me," she said. "Everyone else in my life wanted something else. I was never good enough for my dad. He pushed me so hard, I felt like I never did anything right. Mom, she ran away and now comes back out of the blue, only to want more out of me too. Why are you different?" She turned to me.

"You're anything but a disappointment," I replied. I wished Mel could see her worth the way I did. I wished she never had to play the tough act or wear a mask to feel confident.

"You know that's not true. You know I hurt you, and I'm sorry. I'm so sorry I pressured you, and I'm sorry I caused a rift with you and your parents and I'm sorry you got caught in this whirlwind of my life."

"I really wish you'd stop doing that," I spoke softly.

"Doing what?" She tensed up.

"Apologizing for things you can't control." I turned on the lamp at my bedside to see her mascara was messy. It was supposed to be the best night of her life, and she was here, in tears, standing in front of me.

She was feeling a lot of things, and I knew she didn't quite know how to express them. I knew right then she needed softness more than anything else, even if she wasn't the type to ask for it. I took her hand in mine and we sat down on the side of my bed.

"You've been through so much," I said.

"It's always something. Something good always happens, then it just feels like the world takes it away from me." She looked at the floor. "The world always makes me feel like I'm never enough. That I'm never worthy of stability, of fairness, of love."

"No." I wiped tears away from her face. "That's not true at all. You just had an entire audience screaming at the top of their lungs."

"That might be true." She looked at me. "But you still didn't answer my question."

I squeezed her hand gently and thought: *Be true.*

"Do you remember when you taught me what spooning was? And when I freaked because I thought it was something dirty?" I giggled. "Or the times when we argued about the hierarchy of chip flavours at grocery stores? Or when you taught me how to skip rocks for the first time?"

A small grin formed on her face.

"Do you remember the nights we just got lost, not really keeping track of which roads we went down? And when you taught me how to dance without judgment? I always seen you as the punk rock girl who's sometimes too cool for me, and I don't even care if you like pineapple pizza."

Her smile got a little wider.

"Heck, you even punched my bully in the face in grade ten."

"Lewis was such a prick," Mel said under her breath.

"You deal with my corny pickup lines and still give me butterflies, and you're not afraid to feel as human as you need to. I keep our prom photo on my desk, and whenever life gets too hard, the moments I think about most are the times me and you hold hands and drive down random streets at night. All the highways we drove down and all the adventures we've gone on. I hope you know there's no place I'd rather be than with you," I told her. "There's so many reasons why I love you, for who you are, not what you are, and every moment we share space, I find a few reasons more. What can I say? Maybe Geminis aren't so bad." I grinned.

She laughed out loud. It was the first time I heard her do that in a while, and it put my heart at peace.

"You really didn't have to show up tonight." She rested her head on my shoulder.

"I wanted to." I looked at her. I really needed her to hear this next part. "Mel, I know you have a past, and I know sometimes life can be hard to handle with that trauma. But I always want to remind you that none of that defines who you are. There's nothing I would change about you, Melody. You are the most passionate, generous person I know, and for the moments when you think otherwise, I want to be very clear: You are worthy of love. You always have been, and I promise you that you always will be." I hugged her. She returned it by giving me a tight squeeze.

"Adrian . . . thank you for being you."

"I'm vaguely o —" She pressed her finger against my lips before I could finish and pulled me close. Her lips met mine, and I closed my eyes. The anxiety made its way outside of my chest, and was replaced with her warmth that felt like magic. She leaned into me until we fell back onto the bed.

"We both know you're more than that." She turned the lights off.

CHAPTER 16
Silver Lining

If I learned anything my first week as a university student, it was that frosh week wasn't worth the hype.

Since we arrived, Donny had been on a quest to help me dig deep and find school spirit. He had taken me to meet-and-greets, pancake breakfasts, poetry slams, scavenger hunts, basketball games and obstacle courses around our new campus. Unsurprisingly, I wasn't sold. I just found it exhausting. We hadn't even been in Cape Breton for more than a week. Classes didn't start until Monday, and folks were still moving in, meaning that every time Donny and I went into the hallway, someone, somewhere, was bringing in a couch, mini fridge or large television. I found it crowded and overwhelming. I woke up late that morning feeling hopeful about the Black Student Unity Brunch at the campus lounge. On the surface, Cape Breton seemed pretty . . . white. Donny and I hadn't seen any other Black students around besides Shay as of yet, but I was hopeful and really nervous.

I made my way inside the campus lounge and noticed some students at the far end, near the stage where they held poetry slams and live music. It didn't take me long to hear people laughing and roasting folks.

"So how'd these two clowns make up for profiling you and your homie?" a woman asked.

"We made them order us reparation nachos," Donny retold the story while the students around him laughed.

I laughed too, which led to Donny catching eyes with me. "Adrian! Over here!" He waved, and I made my way over.

"This is my day one, homie. Adrian," Donny introduced me.

"Oh . . . so that's Adrian, huh?" a dude who looked our age said.

"His reputation must precede him," Donny replied, patting my back. "He's a dope guy, did a lot of community work and got a really sick scholarship."

Their eyes looked toward me. I really wished that wasn't the first thing Donny said about me.

"That's awesome! My name is Jackie." The woman nodded at me. "That's Luke." She pointed to the man. He gave me a head nod with a stare.

"Nice to meet you." I sat down.

"So, what are you studying?" Jackie asked.

"I'm in community studies." I tried to be sly.

"Whoa, me too." Jackie smiled. "I just got here from Truro yesterday."

Maybe there was a silver lining to being here. *Who knows?* I could try to be somebody new. Jackie and I already had something in common, and I could just leave the other baggage behind in Halifax to enjoy this new freedom.

"Hey what's going on, Luke?" My thoughts were interrupted by a familiar voice that crept up behind me. *Shay.* I saw him fist pound Luke, then they both looked at me. *What's going on?*

"You two know each other?" I asked, confused.

"Considering Luke is my roommate, we're pretty acquainted." Shay raised an eyebrow.

"Heard a lot about you, Adrian," Luke said in a not so impressed voice.

Shit. I wondered what rumours Shay had passed around about me.

"Mostly good, I'd assume . . ." Donny began to clue in.

"If you call ruining someone's party, leaking private files, and hacking a Facebook group good, I guess so."

Donny did most of that, but I was being blamed.

"Wait, you did what?" Jackie's tone shifted.

"It's a long story . . ."

"Yeah, a long story that ruined my reputation." Shay crossed his arms. "Donny was in on it too," he told Luke.

Donny cut into the awkwardness with a loud laugh.

"Not funny, Donny." Shay's eye darted at him.

"Oh, Shay. I think you're hilarious." Donny returned the energy.

I felt my heartbeat speed up. I didn't want any of this drama. I wanted something new, a low profile.

169

"Hey, I'm gonna try to buy some textbooks before the afternoon." I got up just wanting to get out of there.

"Must be nice. I'm hoping to get some used," Jackie said, not making eye contact. I didn't know how to reply, so I left without saying anything while they stared.

★ ★ ★

I hid away from the world in my dorm room. I knew I should have been out there making friends, meeting new people, but I was worried about what Shay might have already told them. Later that afternoon, Donny slid in the door. He threw his backpack across the room and it landed in front of my bed.

"God, I love university." He picked up his PlayStation controller.

"Class didn't even start yet." I rolled over while he set it up.

I hopped off my bed and grabbed the other controller sitting on the futon we got at a yard sale.

"Still a great day," Donny said while selecting his fighter. "You made quite the exit at lunch."

"Yeah. Because I'm sure Shay is already telling everyone all my secrets." I sighed.

"Yo, forget what Shay thinks." Donny shrugged. "Anyone who listens to him is a clown."

"Only we know he's a clown." I sat up. "He can be a whole new person here, create a whole new persona."

"Yeah, and so can you," Donny pointed out.

"Unless he spreads things about me." I put the controller down and sighed.

"Don't let him." Donny paused the game. "You just have to take some advice from me."

"Meaning?"

"You're coming to a frosh week party with me tomorrow night."

"Frosh week? You can't be serious?"

"I'm completely serious." Donny grinned. "Now follow me."

Donny and I stood in the bathroom of our dorm room, and he began showing me the magic of beard oil. "You put this on your face and hair is going to grow."

"All I ever grow is stubble." I shrugged.

"It'll help it grow in thicker. It's been doing wonders for me," Donny replied, showing off his slightly thicker stubble. I sighed and applied the oil to my face. I didn't understand why Donny had taken an interest in my facial hair.

"Next we need you to get a wardrobe update." He looked at my hoodie.

"What's wrong with this?"

"Too simple. It doesn't make a statement. You need something to stand out." He handed me a black sweater. It was totally his sweater.

When I put it on, it felt way too tight.

"Is it supposed to be this tight?" I asked, standing in front of the mirror, basically showing off my stomach and excess skin.

"It shows you off." Donny patted my back.

"Shows what off? My non-existent six-pack abs?" I grabbed my stomach.

Donny sighed. "I was hoping to save this for you until Christmas, but we have an emergency here." He went through his duffle bag.

"Close your eyes. Open your hands," he ordered.

I did and felt soft fabric on my palms.

"Open up," he said.

I hate Donny so much sometimes.

"You can't be serious?" I shook my head while doing up the last button of a short-sleeved shirt filled with pineapples.

"Trust me, bro. You look awesome. It gives you more personality than a hoodie does, way more than . . . what you had before."

"Donny, why are you suddenly interested in my appearance? There's nothing wrong with the way I dress."

He raised an eyebrow and took a breath.

"It's not that there's anything wrong with what you wear. It's just this is a different place; you can meet new people, be anyone you want, put in a little more effort and maybe impress someone new?"

"Impress someone new? What are you talking about?"

"Listen, you've been super emo since we left Halifax. I know you're missing a piece, and I know that piece is her and . . ."

"Here we go." I rolled my eyes. It hadn't even been a week, and Donny wanted me to move on. It's not that easy.

"I know what you're thinking: way too soon. Maybe it is? But that doesn't mean you can't have a little confidence, or a little fun. That girl you were talking to, Jackie, seemed really cool. She's gonna be at the party."

"Stop." I shook my head. "Maybe I just want to take things slow for a change? It's still fresh, and I need to process it, y'know?"

"Yeah, you're probably right," Donny replied.

Was having a little time too much to ask? Who knows what Cape Breton would bring? I was allowed to take things slow. I deserved that.

"Anyway, we need to get groceries. So let the store aisles be your runway."

Before I could reply to that outrageous sentence, my phone began ringing. It was Dad. I wasn't in the mood to talk to him. I was still sorting out my thoughts and feelings about everything that happened. It wasn't something I could rush or forget about. I just needed time.

"You gonna get it?" Donny asked.

I put my phone on silent. I couldn't stomach talking to Dad, not after everything. I needed space away from him. Maybe that was part of the silver lining. I had space to work things out on my own, without any expectations.

"You'll have all the time in the world to talk to him. Don't worry about it." Donny clued in while putting on his jacket. "On the bright side, you know what they say? Every great love story begins in the Ethnic Juice Aisle."

"Donny, no one has ever said that. Ever." I grabbed my coat.

★ ★ ★

The next night, I found myself at an unofficial frosh week party. It was at a house not too far from the campus. I wasn't really in the mood to go, but Donny already made the choice for me. I leaned against the wall, chewing on a plastic cup, realizing it didn't feel all that different from the shows I'd been to in the past year. Except this time, it didn't really feel like I had much of a reason to be there. I looked across the room to see nobody on the other wall smiling at me. I'd be lying if I said Mel wasn't on my mind.

"Adrian, are you drinking air?" Donny slid beside me, punching my arm. "Come with me." He grabbed my shoulder before I could reply and walked over to the punch table.

"Try this!" He grabbed my cup and poured red liquid in it.

"What is this?" I took a sip. "Ew, what the hell."

"Just drink it. It'll help you loosen up." He grinned, patting my back extra hard. "I think you should go talk to Jackie."

"Jackie? Why?"

"Because I talked you up, and told her that, well, you're available." Donny smiled.

"Donny . . ."

"Come on, man. Please, give it a shot. She's cute, really awesome and I told her you'd talk to her. Maybe you can leave a better impression?"

"You told her I'd talk to her?" I asked, annoyed. I got down the rest of the punch and poured in some more.

"Don't get too loaded," Donny said as I walked away.

Jackie was really cute. But I still wasn't over Mel, even if Donny wanted me to be. I didn't want to keep Jackie waiting either, so I slid over to her with a drink in my hand.

"Hey, Adrian." She smiled at me.

"Hi, Jackie." My face was already red, so I took a drink to hide my shyness. I caught her looking at my shirt.

"You like pineapples, huh?"

"Uh . . . not really, no," I explained. "It's actually an inside joke with me and my friends."

"Oh," she replied, looking ahead. "Inside jokes aren't really that inclusive now, are they?"

"It's . . . a long story . . . I guess."

"Well . . . it sounds like we're gonna be seeing a lot of each other." She sounded nervous. I wished she didn't. I believed Donny when he said he talked me up. I'm sure he put his own spin on it to make me seem cooler than I was. He probably said I drive a Camaro, that I'm a great musician and that —

"I think it's really great you ran a guys' group back in Halifax. Donny said you spoke to them about a lot of social issues," she said. "And he also gave me some context about what happened with Shay's profile. What you did was pretty cool. People like us don't always get a fair shot. You did what you had to for your community. That matters." She smiled. I smiled too.

★ ★ ★

The music inside was too loud, so we found ourselves on the back deck to tune it out. I learned Jackie put together a girl's club for young women of colour, and she planned to help break barriers for young racialized people who were trying to get into post-secondary education.

"Wow, you're doing amazing things," I said as we sat beneath the stars.

"Thanks, Adrian." She sounded shy. "That means a lot from you."

"C'mon!" I laughed. "I'm not that great. I'm . . ." I paused. *What am I doing? Am I still holding on to some kind of hope between Mel and me? Should I rush into anything?*

"You're what?" She got closer, smiling. Jackie was really beautiful. Her eyes met mine, and I couldn't look away. I got closer too, looking at her lips. My phone started ringing before our lips met.

"You gonna get that?" she asked.

It was Mom. She was probably just worried. I was mad at Dad, but the last thing I wanted was to stress Mom out.

"You look like you wanna get that. I'm not going anywhere." Jackie smiled at me.

"Hi, Mom. What's going on?" I stood up walked around the corner.

"Adrian, what's going on? You haven't picked up your phone since you left Halifax." She sounded concerned.

"I know, I know. I'm just . . . adjusting, I guess."

"Oh, yeah? How's that going?" she asked sarcastically.

"Greaaat," I replied as loud music filled the air behind me.

"Sounds like it. Listen, babe. I know you're okay, but your father is worried about you."

"Yeah, well, maybe he should have apologized for everything."

"He's trying," Mom spoke over me. "He wants to visit, real soon."

"Ugh, seriously?"

"Yes, seriously, Adrian," she replied. "He's been talking about you non-stop, y'know? He just wants to talk."

He was one of the last people I wanted to hear from.

"He wants to come up for the last week of September to drop off some boxes you had to leave behind. Just go to dinner with him afterward. Talk to him, A. I'm tired of men not speaking. This is your chance. Say what you need to say, mean it, let it out and be true," she told me as rowdy people shouted inside.

"Listen, I'll let you get back to whatever it is you're doing. I just need you to talk to him, okay?"

"Okay," I gave in. "Love you."

"Love you too." I could hear her grin. "Talk soon."

Why couldn't Dad just give me the space I needed instead of snooping around up here? Anything less than an apology would be a waste of a trip, and that's something I was going to let him know.

"Adrian?" I heard her voice. "You still around?"

"Mel?" I turned to see Jackie and suddenly froze. *Oh shit oh shit oh shit.*

"Uh, no. I'm not Mel." She laughed nervously. "Name's Jackie. Remember?"

"I'm so sorry, I —"

My voice was cut off by an army of drunk dudes and Donny storming the deck chanting, "Frosh week! Frosh week! Frosh week!"

"Adrian!" Donny fell into my arms. "Dude! I am so happy to be here."

"Donny you're . . . really drunk." I raised an eyebrow, smelling the vodka on his breath.

"Man . . . I kept drinking that punch, and you know I think it might be —" He stopped talking.

"Donny?" I asked, while Jackie patted his back.

His eyes widened, and before I could register what was going to happen, it happened. In front of everyone at the party. It was warm, chunky, and smelled horrific.

"Oh, shit! The guy in the pineapple shirt just got vomited on!" a guy yelled, and everyone started screaming. It shook the entire deck.

"Your Christmas gift!" Donny wailed while I stood there frozen and mortified. People began taking pictures, and the flashes blinded me.

"Donny?" I stepped back, moving my arms apart. "What the hell!"

"You two need a drive back to the dorm ASAP. Donny, keys. Now. Let's go!" Jackie pulled me and Donny away.

This new beginning wasn't exactly off to a great start, and this wasn't exactly the silver lining I was looking for.

CHAPTER 17
Settling In

Everybody remembers the guy who got vomited on during a frosh week party. *Everybody.* Donny took it in stride, but I couldn't. Why couldn't I be more like him? It had been a few weeks and classes had started. Sure, nobody outwardly said anything like, "Hey, didn't Donny vomit on you?" But I knew their eyes were lingering, and I could hear the small laughs. A few people posted it on Instagram, and even though my face was blurred out from the flashes, people still seemed to recognize me.

Self-doubt filled me to the brim. Not just from the party. I was beginning to think university wasn't what I had expected. Sure, the classes were interesting. I just couldn't stomach sitting in a lecture hall for three hours. I missed working in the community, with teens, online and offline.

Because of my horrible first impression at the frosh week party, I tried hiding away in my dorm until everyone forgot about me being vomit kid, but Jackie didn't let me do that. After class, she dragged me to the campus lounge to write down some ideas for an assignment. We had a couple papers so far, and were still waiting to see our grades. In the meantime, we were given a paper that wasn't due until January. The instructions were simple: Write the story you're afraid to share. The premise was easy. We have to get to know ourselves before we can really help someone else. It made sense, I guess.

"So . . . you know what you're gonna write about yet?" Jackie asked, sitting across from me.

"I have a few ideas. What about you?"

"I was gonna write about the time I stood up against the school board. They were trying to put forth some sexist dress code, so me and a group of students skipped class and marched the hallways and main office for a month and a half." Jackie laughed. "I guess it was the first time I learned about advocacy, and it paid off."

"That's so dope." I smiled.

What happened between Jackie and I got sidelined. It might have just been in the moment, or the liquid courage Donny filled me up with, but I wasn't really looking for anything. I was still feeling a little sad about —

"Maybe you could tell the story about how you helped Mel and her band." She noticed the surprised look on my face. "Listen, I lurked you on Facebook. I know you and Mel were a thing not too long ago. It is what it is."

"Wow. You're really straight to the point." I took a breath.

"It's just who I am, and what you did matters. It's a hella awesome story if you plan to share."

"Yeah, well, I don't feel great about every part in retrospect." I still felt guilty about what we did to Shay.

"But you could edit out a few details."

"Transparency is important, even when we talk about the stuff we aren't proud of." I wanted to be honest.

"You'll figure it out." She smiled at me, opening up her textbook. "Anyways, you ready to study some psych readings?"

"I'm up for it. This Freud guy had some wild ideas." Before I could grab my textbook, a waiter came over to our table.

"Hey, we're just about to start our monthly poetry slam. Would y'all like to be judges?"

"Uh . . ." Jackie paused and looked at me. "Poetry isn't my thing. Anywhere else we can study?"

The place started to fill up, and I knew some of the folks recognized me from the party.

"Let's head back to my place." I grabbed my bag anxiously.

★ ★ ★

We went back to the dorm hoping to quiz each other on some psych readings to make sure we were actually paying attention to the content. I knew Dad was supposed to be visiting that day to drop off some of my things. I just didn't know when. What was I going to say to him? *"Hey Dad, how's it going? Wanna stick around and watch the fights tonight?"*

"So . . . you and Donny keep this place pretty neat," Jackie said sarcastically as we walked by a laundry pile on the floor.

"That's mostly Donny's stuff," I lied.

"Right." She sounded unconvinced.

Donny had a bunch of homework piled on his desk, unorganized, but he'd somehow made a system that worked. He'd done great on his assignments so far. Across from Donny's desk was mine. I had my laptop, a notebook and —

"You still have a picture of her?" Jackie asked, seeing it on my desk.

"Uh . . . no." I put it face down.

"C'mon, you don't have to be ashamed of it." She laughed, picking it up. "Where was this taken?"

"That photo?" I took it back. It was Mel and I sitting on the swings at the Pit, before we had to worry about the rest of our lives, and having to magically know all the answers to the future. "This was taken last summer at a park by my house called the Pit. I had just started working with Bobby after he launched Unpacking Masculinity, and Mel had gotten back from a provincial tour. She was showing me her new camera and couldn't stop talking about the Cabot Trail."

"It's beautiful. Did you see it yet?" Jackie asked.

"Uh . . . no," I told her. "I was gonna wait until the fall, to see the leaves change colour. That's what we were gonna do, but . . . we never did."

"Oh," Jackie sounded disappointed. "I'm sorr —"

"It's fine." I faked a smile. "Let's get to studying."

While Jackie was reading a case study out loud, I tried

getting my mind off the memory. I grabbed my phone to check Facebook. The first thing I saw on the newsfeed was a photo from Jade with the entire band, arms all around each other, smiling and standing in front of Kara's van. The description read:

Tomorrow is the big day: we're heading on our first NATIONAL FREAKING TOUR! YouTube covers to this!? Pinch me.

"Adrian?" Jackie said. "Are you listening?"

"Yeah, what's up?"

"Based on case four, does that scenario support nature or nurture?"

Before I could answer, there was a knock on the door. I knew it wasn't Donny. He never knocked.

I got up, bit my tongue and opened it.

"Hey, A!"

"Dad . . ." He went in for a hug. I didn't hug him back.

"How ya doing? You liking it here so far?" He smiled and looked over my shoulder.

"It's fine . . ." I took a breath.

"Hey . . ." Jackie squeezed by us. "I'll text you, Adrian." She threw her bag around her back and left.

"It's been less than a month and you're already a ladies' man," Dad whispered. "What'd I tell you?"

I really wish he didn't say that.

"How's living with Donny?" He stepped in and looked around.

"It's definitely . . . interesting," I replied, seeing him look at the posters on the wall.

"Cozy . . ." Dad obviously wasn't impressed. "C'mon. Let's go grab some food. You know any diners?" he asked.

"Willies does all-day breakfast. They're five minutes away."

★ ★ ★

When we got to Willies I ordered toast, bacon and eggs and Dad ordered French toast.

"It must feel like a big upgrade from high school, huh?" Dad asked in a hopeful tone, trying to spark conversation.

It was a huge change from high school. I felt a little intimidated being in lecture halls and bigger class sizes. I knew we were just getting started, but I missed doing the work with Bobby. It'd be awhile before I would have that opportunity. I honestly felt kinda . . . trapped. I didn't want to tell him that though.

"I guess so," I said without making eye contact. "I'm meeting people who are like-minded, at least. That probably wouldn't happen in the other program." I was smug.

Dad shrugged and looked down at his French toast. I wished he didn't have to drown it in maple syrup.

"It is what it is," he replied. "At least you're motivated about something."

"I always have been," I told him, sternly.

"So, tell me about that girl," Dad grinned, changing topics.

"Her name's Jackie." I rolled my eyes. "We're in class together. We were just studying."

"She's pretty cute," Dad pointed out. She was. Jackie was totally awesome, however, I'd put a strict boundary on dating not being a priority while at university.

"I knew you'd be okay. I know you and Mel were together for awhile, but girls come and go. Maybe you can find someone more motivated."

"More motivated?"

"You know what I mean, someone who has a solid plan for the future." Dad doubled down while taking a big bite out of his toast.

"Excuse me?" I dropped my fork. I couldn't believe he didn't get it. "How isn't she motivated?"

"Here we go." Dad rolled his eyes.

"Say what you mean." I was eager to hear his reasoning. Even if we weren't together, I didn't want to hear Dad badmouth Mel.

"Come on, A. Of course she was motivated." He sighed, shaking his head. "I know you miss her, but you need to move on. There's so much more for you out there. I loved that girl too. I just don't know if she was good for you."

"And you are?" I asked. "Did you really drive up here just to say that?" I said way too loud as the waiter refilled our water.

"That's not the only reason I came up here. You need to understand there are bigger, better things on the horizon. You just need to have trust it'll come in the future."

If he thought driving up to Cape Breton and buying me dinner was enough to bury the hatchet, then he was wrong.

"Adrian. I came up here to settle things between us. I'm tired of fighting. Being a father is a responsibility you don't understand."

"That's not good enough!" I cut him off. "You can't just say this isn't something I'd understand. You wanna know what I understand? You avoid conversations when it's tough. You try to bury things instead of apologizing. You say you want to be present when you only offer me distance." I took a breath.

Dad didn't reply.

"Dad. When I lost weight, went through my eating disorder, afterward all you did was show me off without considering how broken I was on the inside." I was honest. Those were painful times, and all he did was tell the world how proud he was of me. "You said the walls in our house were thin, but the thickest walls between us have always been silence. And right now, I need you to listen."

He looked into my eyes.

"This is no different than what Mel's parents put her through."

"Oh, don't go there, Adrian. We never mistreated you." Dad looked upset. "We just wanted the best."

"And so did Martin, so did Prisha, and look what happened. She's running off, away from her parents. At least she won't hate herself after everything is said and done."

"You need to learn to sacrifice. I've sacrificed a lot in my life for you, your mother, our family. Now we're here, and it's your turn to make those same sacrifices for your future."

"I get it," I cut him off. "There's a time when we have to move on. But was it too much to think that maybe I wasn't ready? My friends aren't perfect, and they'd be the first to tell you. They were also the first to never shy away from me when I needed them. They always picked me up, dusted me off and offered me love, even in the moments when I didn't feel worthy of it. Sacrificing them to make you proud makes me wonder if you even cared about me in the first place. Because they loved me for who I am, and you're only proud of what I can become. I already know what I am." I finally let out, "I'm worthy of the life I want to lead."

★ ★ ★

Neither of us finished our meal. Instead, we were left with a silence that carried us for the rest of the trip. When Dad pulled up on the curb outside of the dorms, he pulled out his keys and looked at me. "Adrian, when I got that call from the admissions office, I was beyond excited. I was excited because I . . . I never had that chance."

"I can't be what you couldn't."

"I just want the best for you, along with that scholarship. I know you can do great things. I should have let you go at your pace. I should have —"

"Be well, Dad." I climbed out and made my way to the dorm.

CHAPTER 18

Skipping Rocks Across the Stars

I couldn't believe Dad tried to come and fix things by buying me dinner. What the hell was wrong with him? I was beyond pissed and just needed to breathe. I rushed back out of the dorms and down a path I hadn't seen before. It brought me through the woods as the sun disappeared. I could feel my phone ringing and didn't bother to answer. It was probably Mom asking how it went. I didn't want to talk about it. I just followed the path, and it eventually led me to a lake.

It looked a lot like the lake outside of Mel's cabin. The one we spent so many nights in, away from the rest of the world. Seeing it allowed me to exhale. The first time we went, she made fun of me because I didn't know how to skip a rock across the water. Now my heart was racing from what happened with Dad, so I closed my eyes, thinking back to a happier time, to a better memory from two years ago.

I could almost hear her voice.

"When I was a kid, my mom told me I was magic because I could skip rocks across the stars. Try it," she had told me. It was after a good day. We shared some honest, hard truths, and we went for a drive. Away from the city. Away from school. Away from teenage angst to a place where we could just be with each other. She didn't tell me where it was. She just told me to trust her. I did, and she showed me the cabin for the first time.

I opened my eyes to the present and picked up a rock. I remembered to flick my wrist at the end and watched it skip on across the water reflecting the stars. I remember the morning after: we woke up early to chase what was left of the night sky. We cranked up the music and listened to the songs beneath the stars, chasing a new light, a new day, a future together. Every rock I skipped took me further from that moment. I didn't want nostalgia to be a million miles away. I didn't want those good times just to be memories. I wanted them to be *now*. I sat on a giant rock with my head down. Before long, the stars made themselves comfortable in the sky, and I heard a familiar voice.

"Adrian." I looked to my left and saw Donny come up the path. "There you are."

"Donny, how'd you find me?" I dropped the rocks in my hand.

"I tried calling. You weren't in the dorm room, café or student lounge. I was planning to check out this path anyways. How did things go with your dad?"

"Just another argument."

"Oh," Donny replied, taking a seat next to me. "You look stressed, man." He placed a hand on my shoulder.

"That's an understatement." I shrugged while looking off into the distance. Why couldn't Dad just apologize instead of trying to justify every shitty thing he's done to me? Why didn't he ever show up when it mattered? Why did he think he could decide which direction my life should go? The questions raced through my head, and I didn't know what else to tell Donny besides: "My Dad and I never really had much of a relationship outside of the little things."

I grabbed one of the rocks I'd dropped and threw it into the water. It sank.

"What do you mean?" Donny asked.

"He was always a go-getter, a sports guy, physically strong, while I was always somewhere in-between shy and soft. I think because of that, he saw me as weak."

"You're one of the strongest people I know," Donny replied, tossing a rock too.

"He doesn't see that. I can gather all the strength I have, and he still makes me feel like I'm just a kid. I was always scared of not rising to the occasion because he set standards that were too high and I always felt like I let him down. I'm not the man he wants me to be." I looked at Donny.

"I think a lot of us can relate to that."

"But most dads want their sons to find themselves, not just carry what was set on them. All he wants is for me to do this thing, so he can say I did it. Just like when I lost weight, all he did was show me off. He never checked in on how I was really doing." I let out a breath. "Donny, I thought I knew what I wanted. I thought this was exactly where I wanted to be. I'm starting to wonder if I was wrong? What if I can't carry the weight of the world on my shoulders? What if me and Mel were supposed to explore a new home along the way?"

"What are you going to do about it?"

"Skip rocks." I threw another. "Do you remember when Mr. Price told us going to university was a responsibility? Not just for us, but the community around us. He singled out me and Shay because we got the scholarship," I said.

"Yeah, I remember," Donny said. "It was the last day of school."

"Well, look at the work I did . . . with Bobby at the library, and my online advocacy for eating disorder recovery. I even helped take down some racist music festival," I reflected. "Everything I've already done has been for the community. Why does a scholarship and immediately rushing to university matter more than any of that?" I looked down. "This is what I want to do in the future, but why does it have to be right now? The more I'm rushed, the more I think I'm not ready." I spoke my truth. It was a truth I spent the better part of the summer running away from, thinking that maybe if I embraced everything the world said I should be, then I would embody it. I realized that isn't always the case.

Becoming the person I needed when I was younger didn't change the fact that I'd needed someone when I was younger. Sure, I had adults who were supportive, but maybe I just needed my dad. And he wasn't there.

"No matter how hard I try to tell myself I'm ready, my insecurities surface. Healing isn't linear by any stretch. What if I just need more time?"

"Adrian, time is on your side." Donny skipped another rock. "Maybe the scholarship wasn't exactly a blessing. Having the pressure of the entire community on your shoulders can also be a curse, and now I see that," Donny confirmed. "You've been carrying yourself pretty heavy lately. Since the party, your head's been down, you've been quiet, you've been hurt. I hate seeing you like this, man."

I was glad Donny had picked up on it. Beyond feeling the weight of everything, I couldn't help but feel guilt. I promised Mel I would stay here, and I thought I would be happy, but I was more drained than anything else. What really changed from high school? Frosh week taught me that maybe it wasn't much. Every night I stayed up feeling guilty, wondering "what if" and "what could have been."

"You know she leaves tomorrow, right?" he asked.

"I know." I looked up at him. "She always used to say she had the space for me, if I wanted it."

I wish the world didn't have to bend, shake itself and take us away from one another. When I thought of the future, I always thought of her being part of it.

"Maybe you should let go?" Donny shrugged.

"I can't just let her go." I looked over and saw a grin on his face. "I don't understand what's so funny."

"I'm not talking about her."

★ ★ ★

192

"You're lucky I have two energy drinks in me right now." Donny hit the gas as we got onto the highway.

We had filled a suitcase, jumped in Donny's car and darted off back toward Halifax. I was sitting in Donny's passenger seat, filled with both anxiety and excitement. Maybe my future was in the distance.

"You might wanna text her," Donny told me while switching lanes.

I checked my phone to see it had no reception, and that it was at two per cent.

"Uh-oh, no reception. What about yours?" I asked frantically.

"Back at the dorm. There's no going back now." Donny hit the gas a little harder.

This was a long drive we were getting into, and it was already past midnight. I could only imagine that the band was leaving early, so there were no pit stops. "So . . . if you do this, you know it means no more scholarship, right?" Donny asked.

"I know the risk," I replied.

"Well, I'm glad we have that part figured out," he said.

The one thing I should have known all along was that time was on my side. Regardless of where I end up, I have time to explore before I decide what's right for me.

We had to take a few minutes to stop for gas midway there. Donny parked at a station outside one of the exits and started filling up the tank. When we slowed down, the doubt began to catch up with me.

"You got that look on your face." Donny startled me as he got back in the driver's seat.

"What look?"

"Like you're not sure of yourself." He downed another energy drink, wiped off his face and looked straight at me. "This is what you wanna do, right?"

"Of course it is," I said. "I'm just thinking about what could go wrong here. Dad's gonna be pissed. Mom too. And this scholarship would be meaningless and —"

"Forget the scholarship!" Donny yelled in a caffeinated voice. "Listen, I know I said what I said back at the show after we got profiled. About throwing the scholarship away for this. Then finals night happened, and the way we tore that place down. The way we took up the space, reclaimed it, that's when I finally got it, man. And being part of that is so worthwhile. If you really wanna take a year off, find whatever place you need to be, that's okay. Don't let anyone tell you different anymore. This is your story, and this is your path to follow."

"Thanks for that, Donny."

"Don't get sentimental yet." He hit the gas.

★ ★ ★

The sun began to break through the night as we were nearing Halifax. I was anxious, scared and worried about everything. Donny slowed down when we made it back to the city. It was close to six in the morning, and I could tell he was tired.

"Do you need a coffee?" I asked.

"Caffeine can wait," Donny replied as we drove past the shopping centre. "We're so close."

It didn't take long to get to Queen's Avenue, and I was so relieved by what I saw.

"Mel's car is still there!" I yelled as Donny parked across the street from the purple Camaro. She had to still be home. I tore off my seat belt, grabbed my suitcase and leaped out of the car.

"Go, go, go!" Donny pointed to the door.

I darted up Mel's doorsteps and knocked too hard and too loud for a six a.m. visit.

"Please be here," I whispered. "You have to be here."

The door slowly opened, but it wasn't Mel who I was met with. It was . . . Prisha.

"Adrian?" Prisha was in her housecoat. "What are you doing here? It's six in the morning, and aren't you supposed to be in Cape Breton?"

"Yes. I mean, no. That's not where I'm supposed to be." I caught my breath, trembling at my words. "I'm supposed to be here. I'm supposed to be with Mel."

Prisha clenched her teeth when she realized what was going on.

"Oh, Adrian." Prisha put her hands on her head. "She was right when she said you were a beautiful boy."

"What do you mean? Where is she?" I tried looking past her through the entrance.

She put a hand on my shoulder, took me to the steps and just sat there with me.

"Adrian, she left an hour ago."

"But her car —"

"She left it so the band can save gas money." She patted my back.

"What?"

She left? I tried to say something, anything, but I couldn't. Guilt filled my chest, knowing I wasn't fast enough.

Donny got out of his car and walked up. He looked upset too.

"How long ago did she leave?" he asked.

"She left around five," Prisha told him.

"Shit." Donny ran his hands over his face. "Listen, we can still go after her. I'm sure we could catch up if we floor it. I know for a fact my car is faster than their van!"

Who was I kidding? We didn't know which route, exit or highway they took. We wouldn't even know which direction to go. But that wasn't the only reason we couldn't.

"No," I finally felt brave enough to say. "We can't do that." It would be a waste of time. I knew we couldn't catch up to them, even if I wanted to. It was then I was met with clarity. I had to let her go. As much as I hated to admit it, Dad was right. Sacrifice is a part of life. Regardless of if we feel ready or not. But this was so much more than a scholarship telling me I was ready. It was Bobby, the youth group, even Mel, who made sure I was, and I couldn't let that go to waste. I had to see it through. They believed in me and gave me the strength to believe in myself. That included building the strength to let go.

"Boys, come in for a bit. Refresh yourselves, have some coffee, tea. I'll make some breakfast."

"Thank you, Prisha." I got to my feet.

"Adrian, c'mon, man. We can —"

"Donny, no." It hurt to say, even if I had to.

Prisha let Donny and I hang out for awhile. She poured us coffee, and I had a chance to charge my phone.

"So you were going to throw everything away, for Mel?" Prisha asked, taking a sip from her mug.

"Yeah," I said quietly. I guess in retrospect I should have known they'd leave early. It was a dumb idea. I was so stuck in the moment that I didn't think clearly.

"Wow," Prisha said, letting that sink in. "That's incredibly —"

"Yeah," I sighed, taking a huge sip of the coffee. "I know, it's incredibly stupid."

"I wasn't going to say that," Prisha said. "I was going to say that was incredibly brave, and I wish I had that in me. Melody, she's worth it."

I looked up at her, and I could feel the shared guilt we both carried. The guilt of leaving behind someone we cared about deeply. I could tell we were both really . . . tired. Prisha sat down beside me, giving me a big hug. I hugged her back.

"She's a song," I said to Prisha. "A song that I never wanna forget."

CHAPTER 19
Melody in the Distance

When Mel got back from her provincial tour just over a year ago, she was so restless that we went on a late-night walk to the Pit in the North End.

"You have no idea how energizing it was!" She spun around a streetlight to see me smile.

"From a scale of one to ten, it must have been —" I was cut off by a flash.

"A million." Mel smiled as she took the picture from her Polaroid camera.

"You gonna blind me all night?" I rubbed my eyes, grinning.

"Maybe. I gotta test this new camera out."

"Trust me, Mel. That camera is not new." I laughed while she shook the photo.

"I fell in love with this thing as soon as I seen it in Yarmouth.

I have so many photos from the trip." She showed me the photo of my awkward pose. "I wish you were there."

"Me too." I smiled. "While you were gone, I started doing some work with Mom at the library. I started helping with a guys' group called Unpacking Masculinity. We've been working on important things, making a space where they can be honest and open about themselves. I really wish I'd had a place like that."

"Oh yeah?" She smirked. "I can't imagine the smell."

I laughed. "I was hesitant at first. Junior high students from all across the city come down, and we just . . . talk. Unpack things. Unlearn a lot. In the last session, we spoke about mental health and vulnerability. We shared this in a space that felt honest and full of support. I was skeptical at first, but I'm really enjoying it."

I looked at her to see a big grin on her face. I shook my head. It wasn't funny but it was a lot of fun. It felt special to me.

"What are you smiling at?"

"C'mon, you remember that speech you made? About not wanting to be some kid's inspiration?" She poked my shoulder.

Yeah, she was right. I did say exactly that the year before. It was before everything changed.

"It's not like that." I shrugged.

"It's exactly like that, Adrian Carter." She kissed my cheek. "It's adorable."

"Yeah, yeah, yeah." I smiled as we got closer to the swings, and I hopped on one while she took the other.

Mel had been gone for a month. During that time, I had

gotten to know Bobby a little bit, and the ins and out of working with teenagers . . . I was beginning to feel comfortable doing so.

"Is that the kind of thing you wanna do in the future?" Mel asked as we looked toward the MacKay Bridge.

"I don't know. The future is a long while away."

"I mean, our senior year starts next week," Mel said. "It's coming if we like it or not."

"I know, and Dad's been on my back about it non-stop," I told her. "He's like, you should apply to university early, get a seat reserved, plan out the rest of your life without ever second guessing yourself."

"My dad sounds the same." She shook her head. I knew Martin was always on Mel's back, so I was glad Mel had a little time away from him.

"Well, what's in your future?" I asked eagerly.

"Honestly, Adrian? I think after that trip, I really feel like my future's in the distance, somewhere on the road."

"Oh."

"You sound surprised?" She smiled. "You're acting like I wouldn't have a seat for you."

"Hey, who says I wanna leave?" I was half joking. I felt like everything I wanted was already here.

She didn't reply. Instead she took out a cigarette and lit it up. I wasn't thinking too much about any of that. I just wanted the world to stand still, so I could enjoy the moment as long as possible.

To break the awkward silence, I asked, "So . . . what was the coolest thing you seen on the trip?"

"The coolest thing?" Mel dug in her bag. "This!" She

tossed a Polaroid over to me. I caught it and saw it was a mountain of trees surrounding a path with Jade, Azra and Kara in front of it.

"Where's this?" I asked.

"It's the Cabot Trail, up in Cape Breton." Mel smiled. "It's the coolest place I've ever seen! I want to take you there this fall if we have time."

"Why the fall?"

"Because all those green leaves turn red and it's supposed to be so beautiful." I loved seeing the excitement in her eyes, so I knew it had to be good.

"Well, I'm glad we still have a lot of time." I smiled at her.

"You know I'm gonna hold you to it." She grabbed my hand from her swing.

"Until then, I gift to you, a memory." She took another picture of us.

★ ★ ★

Now, just over a year later, I was holding the Polaroid Mel gave me of the Cabot Trail as I sat on a bus driving through those mountains of red leaves . . . just like Mel said. It was Thanksgiving weekend, but I wasn't ready to go home. I wasn't ready to pretend nothing happened. I also wasn't okay with sleeping in an empty dorm room. So I found myself in White Point, Cape Breton, as the bus pulled off the road in front of the shore. After what happened with Donny and me, we went back to my parents' place. Yes, there was an argument. And now, I wasn't on speaking terms with my dad. Mom tried to help smooth things over. Truthfully, it didn't help. I guess I needed distance to fill the gap.

We still had a lot of the ride to go, so I got out to stretch my legs, walking toward the shore. Ahead I could see the sky touching the sea as the sun began to set.

"You might wanna take a photo," an older woman said as she walked past me. I was probably the only person under the age of fifty on the bus. I didn't overthink it. We all had a lot of reasons for not being with family during Thanksgiving.

"Yeah, you're right," I replied, taking out my phone and capturing the sight. Not as genuine as a Polaroid, but still a memory I wanted to keep. As I went to my home screen, I saw I had a few text messages from Mom, Dad and Donny.

> **Donny:** Hey bro, thinking about you today. I bet you regret not coming to my parents' place for thanksgiving. I'll bring you back a plate
> **Me:** Thanks man, though I'm sure the food will have gone bad by the time you're back lol
> **Donny:** Yeah, u right. More for me

Donny was my brother, and I was grateful to have a friend like him. I just needed some time and space for me. On the trip, I didn't feel the weight of everything like before. I felt like I could enjoy the journey, just for me. I sat down at the edge of the rocks and soaked it in.

As the driver called everyone back to the bus, I noticed an SUV in the parking lot. Beyond the SUV, I could hear arguing. I don't know why I did it, but I was curious enough to make my way past to see someone on their phone.

"All you ever do is tell me I'm not good enough!" I heard the person say. "And if you think working in the city I grew up in isn't good enough for you, then stay gone!" He hung up his phone and threw it into the ocean.

"You go through a lot of phones, don't you, Shay?" I startled him. His look of confusion turned back to anger.

"Adrian, what the hell are you doing here?"

"I'm not here for a fight. I just saw you arguing and wanted to check if you were okay."

"If I'm 'okay?' Since when do you care if I'm okay? After you and your friends —"

"Shay," I cut him off. "It's Thanksgiving weekend. Can we put petty high school drama aside?"

"You hacked my Facebook group!" He raised his voice.

"It wasn't just your Facebook group. It was everyone's, and we used it to make a difference."

"For who!"

"For people who look like me and people who look like you." I pointed at him. He let out a breath.

"I know it may not be my place, but I noticed a message from your dad back at your party, about getting out of Scotia." I sat down beside him. "Why'd you stay?"

"Maybe the same reason you stayed instead of going with Mel and her band. There's value here, even if some folks don't see it."

"Uh . . ." I stammered as Shay raised an eyebrow. "I tried leaving. But . . ."

"It didn't work out and now you're back," Shay finished my sentence.

"It didn't end well."

"No kidding," he scoffed, like he already knew.

"What I'm trying to say is, I kind of know exactly what you're going through."

"Hey, kid! You coming? We're about to head out!" The bus driver called over to me.

I looked at Shay, and he asked, "You wanna grab a coffee or something?"

★ ★ ★

Shay drove to a Tim Hortons drive thru only to stay in the parking lot.

"You know, most people wanna drink their coffee inside," I said from his passenger seat.

"Yeah, well, I don't think the seats inside can do this." Shay pressed a button on his dashboard that warmed up my seat.

"Whoa." I felt my butt get warm.

"Listen, I'm not actually mad at you hacking my group. It is what it is. It was my dad who got mad at me for giving Brown, Black & Infamous a platform."

"Why would he be mad at that?"

"Because my dad is the legal representative of 3AM," Shay said.

"Holy shit!" I almost spilled my coffee.

"Why do you think they'd come to my party in the first place? I just wanted to perform, and I knew if they were there, the place would fill up. Then you guys did what you did."

Guilt filled me to the brim now that I knew what really

happened. I really wished my friends would have responded instead of reacting. And I really wished I'd done more to stop them.

"Anyways, fuck 3AM. They showed up after and trashed the entire place. They were pissed off the band used their gear," Shay said. "So I wasn't mad you hacked the group. I was mad because my dad took it out on me. After Harbor Girls broke up, Dad shifted some of his weight around and made sure 3AM would be involved with finals as a way to keep them from firing him. The organizers thought it'd be easy money too."

Wow. Shay really didn't deserve to carry that burden. If I could take everything back, I would.

"It was rigged from the start, and for what it's worth, I'm honestly glad you helped stop them. Let's just say, my anger at you was a little misplaced, and it took me awhile to figure it out."

"Well, also for what it's worth, I'm sorry we went through your files. I wish I would have stopped them."

"I'm sorry, too," Shay admitted. "Stealing the posters, and you and Donny getting blamed for it wasn't right. I didn't realize how awful that was at first, and I've been feeling terrible about it."

I guess Shay and I weren't as different as I thought.

"I'm guessing you skipped Thanksgiving too?" he asked.

"Yep." I sipped my coffee. "My Dad and I . . . We're not really on speaking terms."

"Did he invite you?"

"Yeah."

"Then know he's trying." Shay pulled out of the parking

lot. "Listen, parents are by no means perfect. I can tell you that. But you have no idea how lucky you are."

"Lucky? You don't know half the story."

"He's still trying," Shay said. "My dad taught me about investing, stocks, business and told me I'm on my own. I never had anyone come visit me, ask me how I'm doing or even give me a chance." That put things into perspective. "Do you know how much I'd give up just to have a father who tried?"

I guess even after everything, Dad was still trying to make things right. Even if I pushed him away time after time, he never gave up on me.

"Parents make mistakes. That's just life. And fixing things can be scary, terrifying even. Maybe he wasn't the best dad in the world, but he's still the dad you got, and he can become better, if you let him in."

I never thought I'd see the day Shay Smith would be throwing wisdom my way. Shay dropped me off at the dorms. By the time we got back, it was late, and the drive made me sleepy. I laid in my bed with my phone open on Dad's contact. I didn't know why I couldn't press call. Maybe I was scared, worried about what he'd say, if he'd be disappointed at me not replying to his texts. My anger was real, valid and honest. Even after everything, he still wanted to try, and a piece of me wanted to try, too. I just couldn't find the strength to hit the call button.

I eventually passed out and woke up to Donny rushing through the door the next morning. A lot of students came back a day early to settle in. I was honestly surprised Donny followed suit.

"How's my introverted best friend doing these days?" He threw his bag on the top bunk. "You know you could have come to my parents' place for Thanksgiving, right?"

"I know. I just wanted to explore the Cabot Trail." I lifted myself up.

"Suit yourself." Donny planted himself in his gaming chair, turning on the console. I was glad Donny got to get away. Things had been awkward ever since we rushed to Halifax.

"By the way, it looks like we have mail," Donny mentioned. "More specifically for you." He tossed an envelope, and it landed on the floor in front of my bed.

"I'm sure it's just an information package from admissions about insurance, credit cards, blah, blah, blah." I laid back down.

"Trust me, dude. That letter isn't from admissions." Donny sounded serious.

I finally got out of bed and picked it up. There was no return address other than saying it was from Montreal. I tore it open to find a letter. It read:

Hey, AC

I really wish I wrote to you sooner. I guess you probably know things have been busy. I imagine you've been busy too. I hope you bought textbooks used and you're not letting Donny keep your place a mess. Sorry to ramble.

If you've been trying to contact me, know that I disconnected my phone. I've been trying to save money on the road, and honestly? It's been blowing up, Adrian.

When it wasn't ringing, it was dead. I think maybe this fame thing is more than I expected.

I don't regret anything. Not yet.

For the first time in forever, I can feel my heartbeat. I can feel the excitement in my chest, and, Adrian, I feel like magic. I feel free, away from the things I felt trapped under. Parental expectations. The world of academia. From hurt. From pain.

I found parts of myself out here that I didn't know existed. I think the best is yet to come.

I don't have an address right now. So writing back would probably be a waste of time. I guess I just wanted to say I miss you. Deeply. If I'm being honest, I didn't think it'd be this hard. I miss your smile, your softness, your really bad pickup lines, your really shitty nachos. I miss you.

I don't know how much hearing this means to you right now, but you've been on my mind a lot. The only thing I want for you is to be happy. I hope you're out there, finding the same freedom that you deserve.

I want to tell you, whenever the wave forms from the monitor of your heartbeat feel like mountains on your shoulders, remember, your name isn't Atlas.

You know exactly who you are, Adrian Carter.

And you already know I'm so proud of you, for all the things you've done, and all the places you'll go. I hope you're smiling somewhere beneath the same stars that I am.

Maybe someday we'll meet again, somewhere in the centre of this universe, beautiful boy.

From the one and only,

— Melody

"You okay?" Donny asked as I put the letter down.

"Yeah." I caught my breath as a tear rolled down my cheek. "I know what I'm going to do." I finally found the strength to let my anger go. I picked up my phone and called Dad.

CHAPTER 20
Press Play

Family is deeper than who we're connected to by blood. Family is measured by who shows up, and who you show up for. Family are those who'll work through issues instead of pushing them aside. And family has always been around me, even if I didn't always see it clearly.

I ended up finishing my semester strong, and I spent Christmas eating a lot of food at home. I planned to go back to Cape Breton a few days early to finish my psych paper. Dad insisted on driving me back.

"You really didn't have to do this. I could have taken the Maritime Bus," I told him as we crossed the causeway into Cape Breton.

"I know, I know. I just haven't seen you lately. I miss having you around the house."

"I miss being there," I said. "But I really like the work

I'm doing now. For a moment, I thought I wasn't ready, and now I feel like I'm exactly where I need to be." Dad and I were working on being more present in each other's lives. When Dad picked up the phone that day, I told him I was tired of fighting. So was he. That meant we had to find a solution. Sure, it was awkward at times. And there was a lot we didn't get right, but we were both willing, and we were both growing.

"A, I'm really glad you came home for Christmas." Dad looked down the road. "I seen how south things went with Mel and her parents. When she caught wind of what I said, and then hearing what happened after. You have no idea how awful I felt." He had a lot of regret in his voice. "What happened with Mel and her parents . . . I don't want that to be us."

"Me neither," I replied, watching the road outside the passenger window.

"I know there are some things I can't take back, no matter how hard I try. The only thing I can do is be better, and I learned that from you," Dad said. "I know there are some kids out there who'll need you."

I smiled, even though I didn't let him see it.

When we rolled up to the dorm, he put the car in park. There weren't many students around yet. Class didn't start for a few more days. I just wanted a little time alone before things sped up again.

"You gonna give me a call on Sunday?" Dad asked.

"Yeah, always." I got out, and he did too. He pulled me into a hug.

"I'm proud of you, you know that, right?"

"I know." I smiled and hugged him back.

"It's just . . . I don't know if I said it enough. I'm really glad you made the decision you did. I'm sorry I . . ."

"I know," I said again. "I'll call you on Sunday."

I was happy to see his grin. I didn't get to see it too often anymore.

"Be safe," he said, getting back in his car.

"Always." I waved as he drove off.

★ ★ ★

I made it to the dorm room, threw my suitcase on my bed and sat at the desk. I pulled out my laptop and opened up the paper I wanted to get done. I usually worked best when I was alone, and it wasn't always easy with Donny around. He was having a great time with his family back home, and I was glad to take advantage of it. I opened the document "Eating Disorders in Black Men: the Untold Struggle," knowing I was no longer afraid to tell this story.

I had gained my freshman fifteen. But I wasn't as hard on myself about those things anymore. I wasn't an active member in the recovery group anymore, but I still checked in once in awhile. They seemed to be doing okay. Other young folks had risen to the occasion as I knew they would. Things had been going pretty good for me. I was smiling a lot more, had made some really cool friends and felt more at home up there in the cold. I had a really great crew: me, Donny, Shay, Jackie and Luke. We were all part of the Black Student Union at CBU. I never would have thought about working with Shay before. One thing

I'd learned was that life was a wild journey. *You never know where you might end up.*

I checked Facebook and saw I'd received a message from Donny.

Donny: Yo man you see this!!?!?!?

It came with a link to an article with the headline "Halifax band Brown, Black & Infamous wins CBC Searchlight Award."

"What! Wow!" I gasped. *The Searchlight Award? That's huge.* I clicked through to the article. It said they had finished their cross-country tour and were set to open up the Junos. I had to say it out loud to believe it. "Whoa." *The world really is theirs, huh?*

If the tour was over, I wondered where Mel had decided to go. She'd told me she wasn't coming back home. I hadn't heard from her in months and missed her deeply, but I was glad she found something new.

★ ★ ★

I spent the majority of the night working on my paper until I fell asleep at my desk. The next morning, I walked down the empty halls, and it was nice seeing the school empty for once. I had to work a shift at Willies later that day. I'd applied there a month earlier, and everyone was super nice, even if being a waiter wasn't the best gig. I needed the money. *Scholarships aren't magic. Every bit counts.* I continued working on my paper for the next couple of days. It had to be about 3,500 words, but I was already at 2,000, so I thought I deserved a little break.

When Sunday evening rolled around, I knew Dad expected that call. I didn't keep him waiting.

"Hey, A." Dad picked up, knowing it was me. "How's it going?"

"I'm still feeling that turkey in my tummy," I said, rubbing my stomach.

"You should have taken more. We still have tons of it here."

"That's the problem. I'd definitely eat all of it."

"Don't worry about that kind of thing anymore —"

"I'm not," I laughed. "I'm joking."

"I get you." Dad laughed back. "Well, let me guess, you regret going back early? Instead of watching some fights with your old man?" I could tell he was smiling.

"No, I'm having a lot of fun. Being in this school. Alone. Walking down empty hallways. Working at the diner," I said sarcastically.

"Don't have too much fun, because I've been thinking —"

"Uh oh," I replied with a grin.

"Hey, don't shun me just yet," he chuckled. "Listen, A. It's about time you learned how to drive. I have some money saved up if you wanna try driving school this summer, and heck, maybe if you wanted a cheap car, I can help. What do you have in mind?"

He was right about that. I spent the better part of my teenage years having other people drive me around. Maybe I could borrow Donny's car once in awhile. I spun my computer chair around to my window to see a . . . "Purple Camaro." My eyes widened.

"Purple what?" Dad asked.

"Dad, I gotta go," I said, hanging up the phone and walking toward my window.

A purple Camaro sat in the parking lot outside.

I put on a coat and my beanie and headed outside, unsure what I was going to find. My heart was beating out of my chest. I walked to the Camaro, and I saw the Brown, Black & Infamous bumper sticker. *She's here.* My shoulders tensed and my throat tightened. I saw some footprints in the snow leading toward the observatory.

I took a breath and walked the short distance as snow fell all around me. I pushed the door open, and it creaked slowly. It was dark, but I had seen a blue light in the distance. I gulped and slowly stepped ahead to hear a riff in the distance. Once I walked through the hall and past the pillars, I looked up and saw her.

Anxiety filled my chest, and I began to climb the ladder to where she was.

"Mel? Mel!" I managed to get out.

"Adrian!" She looked down from the platform high above. Mel was sitting at a computer screen that projected images and maps of anywhere she programmed. She closed it in on Cape Breton. Around her were models of planets, and the floor above had a giant telescope aimed at the sky. I climbed up and she ran over to pull me into a hug.

"Mel. Hi," I said, soaking it in.

"God, I missed you." She squeezed me even tighter.

"I missed you too." I let go as I caught my breath. That's when I finally got a good look. "You . . . you have a . . . septum ring."

"Wow." Mel grinned, then looked me up and down for a moment. "Y'know, I was wondering if you'd try to grow a beard."

I felt the stubble on my face. "Donny gave me some beard oil."

"How's that going for you?" She smirked and turned to the computer. "I wasn't sure which dorm was yours. I was planning on finding it, but I got sidetracked here."

Of course she'd come here.

"Mel . . ." I trailed off. "What are you doing here? I thought you weren't coming back."

"Yeah, me too," Mel replied, not looking my way. Instead, she zoomed out of Cape Breton on the projector, and it expanded into the entire map of Canada. Little icons started lighting up on locations such as Montreal, Toronto, Ottawa, Winnipeg, Saskatoon, Victoria and Vancouver.

"Those are the places you told me you'd go."

"Yeah." She smiled. "We went to all of them."

She must have had a few stories to tell along the way.

"I'm sorry to just show up out of the blue," she finally said. "I don't exactly have a phone right now. I actually tried to catch you at your parent's place, found out you were back here. I told them not to say anything." She looked at me as moonlight splashed across her face. "Do you wanna go for a drive?"

★ ★ ★

"So when we made it to Montreal, we lost Jade," Mel told me as she drove us off the property.

216

"What? How'd you lose her?" I laughed.

"I blame the twenty-four-hour clock. We were supposed to meet at the subway for 13:00, I woke up still half asleep and told her that meant three o'clock, so of course we searched the entire city trying to find her, me feeling awful knowing I should have said one o'clock." Mel giggled at what had happened. "She still showed up at the venue, but wouldn't let me forget it for the rest of the trip."

We both laughed. Poor Jade.

"I heard you guys won the Searchlight Award," I said.

"You read that, huh?" She smiled. "Honestly, I was surprised they chose us."

"Why? You're all amazing. That night in the warehouse, you almost brought the entire place down."

I saw her grin. Mel took a turn off an exit that led us to a path on top of a hill. We got out, and she sat on the hood of the car while I stuffed my hands in my pockets. Below I could see trees for miles, and even if the leaves were gone, that didn't mean it wasn't beautiful.

Mel finally cut the silence and said, "The road can be a healing place if you let it. I found out a lot about myself, my needs, my wants, expectations, self-worth. Adrian, that trip changed me. So, so much."

"I'm glad," I replied. If anyone deserved to heal, it was her. "What brought you back?"

"How have you been?" she asked, avoiding the question.

"I've been good. I came here and I, uh . . . a lot happened. Donny barfed on me at a party, my dad and I got in a bad fight, Shay and I became friends and gosh, this world is a whirlwind that doesn't make sense sometimes."

Her eyes widened. "You're gonna have to put the pieces together here." Mel patted the hood for me to sit next to her.

I pulled up, got close and told her the story.

"I can't believe Shay's dad is such an ass! I actually feel bad for him," Mel confessed. "I'm so proud of you for talking to your dad, and putting in the work."

"Thanks, Mel." I smiled and wondered how she was doing. Did she and Prisha ever make up?

"So, did you see your parents?" I was curious.

"Yes. Well, not together," Mel said. "My mom left Halifax shortly after we did."

"I'm sorry, Mel." I felt really bad.

"Don't be," Mel reassured me. "Our first night in Toronto, I was surprised to see her front row and centre, wearing a Brown, Black & Infamous shirt cheering with the crowd." Mel smiled.

"What? You can't be —"

"I'm absolutely serious, Adrian." Mel sounded like she was on cloud nine. "After the show, she came backstage, and we just talked everything out. And we've been in touch ever since. She said she was inspired by something you did."

"Something I did?" I got nervous.

"Yes. Please don't ever do that again." Mel shook her head at me. "You need to be here, studying. It's going to pay off. After all, the world needs someone like you."

"Someone like me?" I replied, laughing. "Mel, you're performing at the Junos!"

"Maybe the world needs both of us, for different reasons. But I didn't want to come here to talk about myself," Mel said.

"Then what did you wanna talk about?"

"Us," she finally said, looking off into the distance. "I was so sure I wasn't coming back. I made plans to find someplace in Ontario. Honestly, I still might. The band, we're not done. We're only getting started."

"You deserve the best." I smiled.

"When I was on the road, you were never too far from my mind."

It was like everything around me went silent, and I could hear my heart beat like a drum. That was a scary thing about being apart: I wondered if I was ever on her mind, because she was always on mine.

"This sounds really silly." She shook her head. "I was kinda worried that maybe you met someone new. Some-one who made you feel all the ways you deserve to feel. And I would be very happy if you did, but I would be a little sad if that person wasn't me." She blushed. "I was scared you moved on, and I'm not even sure if you have or not. All I know is you're someone worth coming back for, even for a little while."

"Mel . . ." I let out. "I . . . I haven't stopped thinking about you either. I wasn't sure if I'd ever see you again, and I wanted you to be okay. That's what I want most, for you to be okay."

Mel took in a deep breath and closed her eyes. When she opened them, she smiled at me.

"Believe me when I say that I'm okay." She wrapped her arms around me. I felt at ease with a warmth in my chest. It felt nostalgic, and maybe it wasn't so bad. I hugged her back, not wanting to let another one of these moments go.

"I really miss those." She rested her head on my chest.

"And I really miss you." I held on to her tight.

"I'm sorry I hurt you." Mel looked up at me.

"Sometimes we just need a little space to figure things out. I'm sorry I wasn't honest in the beginning."

Mel loosened her grip. I guess she was still processing a lot.

"The band plans to hit the road again sooner than later. I think that's where I need to be, on the road. I need to perform, send a message, talk to the people. I need to be everything I want to be." She turned back to me and said, "I need you to be everything you want to be, too. It's the only way this can work. We're a team." She stopped herself, then said, "I mean, if you want us to be a team. I need you to want that too."

"I do," I replied without hesitation. "I kept thinking back to the last couple years, of all the shows we went to, all the nights we spent driving down any road we could find and all the laughs we shared. It was everything I was ever after. I guess you never really know this is it until it's over, and Mel, I don't want this to be over. I don't want *us* to be over."

She smiled. "Maybe when you're done all your business here, you can hit the road with me. We can find some type of future, together."

"I like the idea about us in the future." I smiled.

She gripped my hand tight. "Until then, I have some time, and so do you. Why don't you show me around the Cabot Trail?" She got a little closer. I was so glad she was back, and I wanted to hear the stories she had to tell.

"We have a night sky above us, a long road in front of us and I have a lot of new songs that I want you to hear," she whispered in my ear, then pulled me in close. Her lips met mine. She kissed me, and I kissed her back, knowing that even if we had missed seeing the leaves changing colour, this was so much better. Her hand clasped with mine, and I closed my eyes. I could hear her melody loud and clear. Her melody was back in the centre of my universe. She pulled my hand, rushing us to her car. I hopped in the passenger side while she started the engine. Her MP3 player sat on the dashboard connected to an AUX cord. I took it in my hand and looked over at her.

I smiled as Mel put her foot on the gas, spinning the car around to drive beneath the stars, knowing the best of us was yet to come.

We locked hands, knowing no matter what the world threw at us, either expectations that were too high or not finding a place to fit, it was fine. The only thing I knew was that we wanted to be together, on this great journey, listening to these songs across the stars, and the truth was, the new journey starts *now*. We weren't just driving down roads, or highways, or alleys anymore. We were off towards a new destination: It was called the future.

"What are you waiting for?" she whispered. "Press play."

Acknowledgements

The Summer Between Us started off as a sequel to my first novel, *Worthy of Love*. Over time, through drafts and rewrites, it became something so much more. It turned into a love letter and a send-off to the characters I first started writing about when I was sixteen years old. Ten years later, I feel lucky enough to have grown alongside them in ways I wasn't sure I could. Being able to explore themes of emotional maturity, resiliency and vulnerability has been a healing ride for me. I hope it has been for you too. It's safe to say goodbyes are hard. Even for the authors.

I want to thank Sarah Mack and the editorial team at Formac Publishing for bringing this story to life. To Wanda Lauren Taylor, for having faith in me as a writer, and knowing there was more to this story. To Meghan Sivani, for being a punk rock encyclopedia and an amazing friend. To Malik Adams and El Jones. We never forget our mentors. Thank you for all you've done. To David Zinck, for pushing me to work with youth. Teenagers aren't as scary as they used to be. Only sometimes. To Saleem Hussain Ansari, thanks for the laughs and the friendship you've shown me. To Sarah Sawler, I appreciate the advice and friendship you've given me over the years. To Sridaya Srivatsan, I'm filled with gratitude for the time and space you gave me during the creation of this novel. I couldn't have done this without you all. Thank you.

With all that being said, it was a pleasure to write Adrian and Mel's journey. We all need a reminder that we're worthy of love, safety and most importantly, the life we wish to lead. We don't get too many stories about kids like them. We don't always get permission to show the best parts of ourselves, or the power to illuminate the hearts around us. All I hope is that the love they share falls into the hands of those who need it, and that the readers can find the strength to become everything they aim to be.

Thank you for being part of this journey.

With endless gratitude,
Andre.